Also by China Alexandria:

The Cuthbert and Bede Series
The Bone Bible
The Infernal Serpent
The Hellfire Club

The Wild Geese Series
Wild Geese
Brazil's Guardians of Evil
Atlanta's Night of the Burning
Miami's Seven Sisters of Evil
Breaking the Millennium Code

THE URBAN CHAMELEON

China Alexandria

Published in 2016 by Arctic Books Publishers
Coppice Cottage, Castle Close,
Tudhoe, Spennymoor,
Co Durham, DL16 6TR

© China Alexandria 2016

China Alexandria has asserted his right under the Copyright, Designs and Patents Act 1988 to be identified as the author of this work.

This book is a work of fiction and any resemblance to actual persons, living or dead, is purely coincidental.

ISBN: 9780995552715 (EBOOK)
ISBN: 9780995552708 (PAPERBACK)

Cover design by Lumphanan Press
www.lumphananpress.co.uk

Evil is at its most threatening when it has been doused and lies inert.

When unwatched and forgotten evil smoulders and waits.

Introduction

VICTOR SWAN DID NOT LIKE MONDAYS, ESPECIALLY WET AND cold Mondays. They always reminded him of the bad old days at the children's home. He looked at his watch and questioned whether it was the correct time, day and cemetery.

Steaming black earth from the freshly dug grave spilled onto the steel hard white frosted grass. After he unbuttoned his overcoat he brushed down the fine feathers from his pullover. It had been a stupid idea to check on the peacocks before leaving, but the thought of his first clutch of home bred eggs had excited him and he had not expected the mother, the peahen, to fly at him.

Just visible now over the camber in the road he spied long black plumes dancing to the rhythmic movement of the four black Welsh Cobb horses. Finally he could bury his father and begin to move on in life.

The carriage driver sat high up on the hearse like a charioteer, droplets of rainwater decorating the brim of his black bowler hat. A Bentley followed carrying the four pall bearers and the small Irish padre. The padre stumbled as he stepped out of the car and struggled to keep his cassock down as it billowed in the strengthening wind.

Victor was pleased when the procedures were finally over, the hasty bible reading, the singing of a hymn and the handful of soil thrown onto the coffin quickly completed before the threatening clouds had burst.

He enjoyed the comfort of sitting in front of the coal fire in the Woodlands Road pub just across from the cemetery, savouring a pint of heavy and a whisky while wearing his father's first and Second World War medals, his military tie around his neck. In truth he had never known his father, being a military man working in code breaking and spending so much time away from home. Victor was surprised that no army representative had attended the funeral; in fact he had been his father's sole mourner.

After finishing his last beer and whiskey chaser he got up to go, his peace and quiet ruined by the porters and nurses from the hospital across the road starting to come in.

He stumbled from the back entrance step into the arms of a local thug.

Victor could see the lips moving and the huge gold tooth flash but couldn't make out a word of what the thug was saying. It was only when his head hit the wet cobbles and he felt the heavy boots pummel his stomach that his hearing returned.

In fact the noise was very loud, getting louder, and when he sat up and put his back against the pub's wall he saw the flashing blue light of an ambulance rushing into the hospital. He struggled to stand but slowly managed to get half way across the street before the long white car hit him.

When he woke he was unsure if he was dreaming or had gone to heaven.

"So you are with us sleepy head?" The young blonde girl said, "Funny that, you coming from the hospital and then getting knocked down."

"I was actually going in to the hospital," Victor said as he rubbed his stomach, "I was mugged behind the pub just across the road."

"How much did they take?" She asked.

"Nothing, I had spent everything in the pub," he showed her the torn ribbons, "but they took my medals."

She looked straight through him for some time and Victor started to worry about her not watching the road as she drove.

"Are you a kind of war hero or some James Bond spy that can't let anyone know your secret?" She asked.

"I can't say that," he said and she nodded, knowing that the real spies don't own up to it.

"I removed your tie and opened your shirt button to get you breathing." She wound the tie around her hand, "What's this funny tie pin?"

"It's a peacock. I just started keeping them and hope one day to start breeding them. I actually thought you were an angel and I had gone to heaven."

Laughing she pulled off her wig and white blouse, leaving her close to bald and wearing an *I Love NY* t-shirt.

"I have different images of myself: *The Office Tart, The Girl at the Pop Concert, The Police Woman.*"

"Police Woman?" Victor repeated.

"It's for my job." She pulled a brass ring from her bag and clipped it onto her nose to complete this image. "I will show you," she went on, as they pulled into Glasgow Airport's long stay car park and drove up and down between the rows of cars.

"Bingo, see the black car further up on the right?" She held up a bunch of keys, "I have a key that fits that car."

"So you don't actually own this car we are in?" Victor asked.

"Do I look like someone who would have a hundred and sixty grand in my purse? This is a Mercedes six hundred, known as the Big One because it has the S Class body and twelve cylinders of German power."

"Maybe not," Victor suddenly looked in the glove compartment and pulled out a long silver pistol.

"Last time I drove this car there was a joke flower in there that squirted water," she said, "maybe the owner sells stage props or is a clown."

As Victor pulled the trigger a flag flew up from the gun with the word 'Bang' on it; they both laughed.

"When passengers park here they put a ticket on the dash with their return date and give the security guard the keys to park the car. Sometimes he leaves them in the car. Can you drive?" She asked and Victor shook his head. "I will take the black car, the Yukon Denali off roader down to the beach and I will teach you," she announced. "What do they call you?"

"Victor, Victor Swan."

"My manager calls me the Urban Chameleon. Do you live in Glasgow?"

"The tower in Bearsden, I keep the peacocks in a big shed at the back."

"Do you like visiting graveyards and reading the tombstones?" She asked.

"What gravestones?" Victor pulled a face and shook his head.

"Sometimes I spend all night reading the names and making up stories, dreaming I am one of the people etched on the stone."

After driving up and down the shoreline of Portpatrick beach they ran into the sea and swam naked in the ice cold water. Afterwards they lay close together on the beach, their bodies entwined, and later Victor closed his eyes and felt alive.

"Are you at one with nature?" She asked.

"For the first time in my life, I think I am."

"To be fully at one you must develop the mind. This is achieved by discipline of the body, following the movements of God's creatures." She stood, poised to express each movement with her body. "From the crane we learn grace and self control, from the snake suppleness and rhythmic endurance. The praying mantis teaches us speed and patience, the tiger tenacity and power. Finally from the dragon we learn to ride the wind. You see Victor, all creatures low and high are at one with nature. If we have the wisdom to learn all animals may teach us their virtues. Between the fragile beauty of the praying mantis and the fire and passion of the winged dragon, there is no discord. Between the supple silence of the snake and the eagle's claws there is only harmony. No two elements of nature are in conflict."

"Do you ever sleep?" Victor asked, feeling sleepy.

"Oh yes, even chameleons sleep. I must get back to my Whacko Hotel. You can keep the car till Monday morning and exchange it for the white one."

Victor drove the coast road up to Glasgow and dropped her off to the rear of what looked like an army barracks. He sat and watched as she slipped through some bushes and through a small gap in a mesh fence and then stood in the doorway.

"Goodbye then," Victor shouted.

"Never say goodbye, say *hasta la vista*, baby." She then held the palm of her hand up to the side of her head, mimicking a pistol, and pulled back her thumb, the hammer, made a "boom" sound and fell through the door.

He stayed at home Saturday and Sunday feeling strange and alone. His life had changed dramatically since his father's death. He had been in constant demand from his father, feeding and cleaning him, changing his oxygen bottle.

He pondered if it had all been a dream, meeting the girl and her turning him into someone else. He put his hand in his pocket to feel the large bunch of keys and looked out of the window at the car, getting excited just thinking about her.

I will take it back early, he thought, *and take her up with me*. Now he was starting to feel really excited.

He pushed through the same bushes she had pushed through and stood at the glass patio door, through which he could see her sleeping, but not a normal sleep, something much deeper. A girl suddenly came into the room and picked up a clipboard that hung at the bottom of her bed, seeing Victor she smiled and opened the door.

"You know Miss Smith, are you a relative?" The nurse asked.

"No, a friend and I have brought something for her." Victor held up the tall white swan, "It's silly really."

"No not at all, since her car accident anything from the past, music or a certain perfume can sometimes help bring them back. I would like you to meet her consultant, Doctor Moss."

Victor waited in a small office while she went for the doctor.

"This is Doctor Moss," the nurse introduced him and they shook hands.

"I don't want to build your hopes up too much but Nurse Fielding observed slight eye movement three weeks ago."

"Slight eye movement?" Victor repeated, confused. He watched as the doctor scanned the cover of each file. There were animal names on the file covers instead of the patient's name. There was a bear, a tiger, or a cow to signify the character of the patient.

"That is her file there at the bottom of the pile, the Urban Chameleon," Victor said pointing.

"Yes," the doctor joked, "I have names for all my patients. She had eye movements on the twenty third but nothing since, so she may never recover."

"Do her parents come to visit her?" He asked.

"We think her father was killed in the same accident and no other relatives have come forward," the doctor closed the file. "She doesn't even know her father is dead. I have just received the Police forensic file on the accident today."

Suddenly there was the sound of a man shouting and swearing coming from the far end of the corridor, the nurse rushed in to the room and the Doctor threw the file down on to the desk, then they both rushed out to attend to the hysterical patient.

Victor Swan had never been curious about anything in the whole of his life. He had seen other boys on school trips looking into rabbit holes, holes in trees and even into shells, curious at what might lurk inside, but Victor had not been interested. Until now. He felt different since he had met the girl. She had unleashed something deep inside.

He could read the large *S* and the words *file under suicide*. He could make out her code name, *chameleon* upside down on the file, but struggled to read her real name underneath. He could see it began with a *U*. He quickly turned the file around and picked it up: *Name Unknown*.

He slid out the photographs of the accident scene. The first showed the girl standing on the hard shoulder of a motorway hitching a lift, the second her climbing into an Oxford Cambridge car. *So,* Victor thought, *he was not her father but simply picked her up at the side of the road*. He now looked at the accident scene photographs and saw the utter carnage.

A wagon and a bus were fused together by the tremendous heat from a fire and a car was embedded into a tree.

Cause of accident: *The girl's fingerprints on the steering wheel of the Oxford Cambridge clearly show a pulling motion, suggesting she had purposely caused the car to veer into the wagon, which in turn hit the oncoming bus. Thirty three people in total died because of her action.*

Victor put the file back down on the table and stood up. He walked out confused and unsure of what to do. He walked the full perimeter of the building and came upon the main entrance, where a huge blue and white sign screamed out the building's name: Carstairs Mental Institute.

Chapter One

Stranraer Ferry Terminal

DETECTIVE INSPECTOR DOROTHY MALONE AND HER SERGEANT George Bede entered the terminal manager's office.

"I am Inspector Dorothy Malone and this is Sergeant George Bede, from Strathclyde police, we are investigating the report of a suspect package." She pulled out her warrant card, as did Sergeant Bede, "We have inspected the 'suspect package' taped crudely to the ferry terminal barrier."

"A young couple, didn't want to give their names, said they saw a tall person over by the barrier acting suspiciously," manager Stevie Nicks said.

"You have a description of this person?" Bede asked, "Male or female?"

"The mist was coming in and visibility was poor, but they filled in a description sheet," he handed it to the Inspector.

"Very tall with dark waterproof clothing and a wool hat," she read out, "He was unsure about gender but she said definitely female."

"Well, woman know these things," Stevie smiled. "I took a look at the barrier and found a package with several wires hanging from it and what looks like a battery so I informed you."

"Thank you Mr Nicks, just leave the bomb to my Sergeant, he will sort it."

"What's this 'my Sergeant will sort it' shit?" Bede exclaimed. "Cuthbert wouldn't have me defusing bombs, he would get the Bomb Disposal Unit."

"The Chief Inspector is on the first day of his holiday and the ferry from Larne is waiting to dock," she said, handing him a small black leather case containing the tools.

"George gently, George, open the casing gently!" Shouted Dorothy Malone, "It may have a shaker device or a hair trigger activator!"

Bede felt as nervous as a thoroughbred while feeling the outer casing, but the use of his first name made him think that Dorothy must be warming to him finally.

"Bede you arsehole, hold it steady!" Her voice sounded even louder carried over the wind, "You'll blow us both up into high heaven!"

"Right, it is open," Bede announced, sweat now trickling down his chin, "Do I cut the red wire or the blue wire Dolly?" Bede asked.

"I am Detective Inspector Dorothy Malone, Sergeant," she answered "and since joining the common market…"

"I don't need a lesson in diplomacy," Bede yelled, "I've got a homemade explosive device six inches above my wedding tackle in a north easterly on Stranraer Ferry Terminal with rain and hail pummelling my face like a collier's pick, so tell me, do I cut the red or the blue wire?"

"Since joining the common market we adopted the international coding system," she repeated.

"Bloody hell!" Bede yelled as he cut through both wires and hurled it to the ground. After a moment Dolly walked over to the device, picked it up and inspected it.

"Bloody amateurs," she cursed, and hurled it into the Irish Sea, just in time for a gigantic boom to ring out across the terminal. Dolly was blown up into the Stranraer night, turned full circle, and landed spread-eagled upon the unsuspecting Sergeant.

Bede felt the full force of her long muscular body as she landed on him. Even though his breathing became strained and restricted, with her six foot seven inch frame on top of him he couldn't help but feel that things were looking up.

Two things he liked about Dolly were her 'perfectly formed headlamps'. He gently put his hands on her chest and slowly eased her off him. He could sense they were on 'full beam'.

"I didn't realise you were so big Sergeant," Dolly whispered.

"I must go back home before we return to the station," Bede said, embarrassed, "I need some, em…"

Dolly could see he was stumbling for the next words.

"Anti-Terrorist Equipment?" she suggested.

"No Detective, clean underpants," Bede replied.

Chapter Two

VICTOR SWAN PACED THE FLOOR, STARING AT THE TELEphone and then at the car sitting in the back yard. He was unsure what to do about the young girl he had met. She had been the first real friend he'd had, and the closeness on the beach was the best, well, the only time he had done something like that with a girl.

He wiped the blood from his hand with a tissue; he had been surprised by how protective the peahen had been guarding her egg. His father was frowning, looking down on him from his portrait above the mantle, "Steer clear of her," he would have said, "she is a woman and women are trouble."

Victor fired up the car knowing he would have to take it back to the airport that night. He considered whether to bring another car back.

As he pulled into the airport's long stay car park he saw her, halfway in and half way out of an army Land Rover. As he approached she turned and he saw she was holding a machine gun.

"Ch, ch ch!" She laughed as she made the sound of the gun firing bullets at him, "It's alright Victor, I emptied the gun doing target practice down on the beach," she threw the gun in the back of the Land Rover and climbed in beside him.

"We want a posh car for tonight. You're taking me to the hotel for a meal as it's my birthday."

"You haven't got any other guns with you?" Victor asked.

"No silly," she laughed. "Only a hand grenade in my secret pocket."

"I have something for you," she handed him a card.

"*Elephants are grey but not all grey things are elephants,*" Victor read the message. "But what does it mean? I don't understand."

"Well, my nurse is a spy like you. She tells me that it's like a kind of code, you say it when you meet up with other spies. Keep it somewhere safe Victor, it is something to remind you of me."

Victor pushed the card into his pocket and was pleased when they had arrived at the Portpatrick Hotel, she had talked non-stop during the journey down. It was her white gloved hands that he had watched though, *What if she starts pulling at the wheel?*

She looked like a queen as she walked through the hotel's main door wearing a sky blue jacket and a white tennis skirt with calf-skin boots. He took her coat and she sat down at a table while he went to the bar to order drinks and their meals.

"Can I take your name sir?" The tall Oriental girl asked.

"Victor Swan," he announced.

Out of nowhere a bus load of Japanese tourists came in and within seconds the birthday girl was behind the bar helping to serve drinks. The small blonde hotel manageress raised her hand and high-fived, showing she obviously knew her.

Victor sat alone eating his meal. He looked up to see the chameleon rushing at one of the tourists, scratching his face. Victor and the manageress managed to pull her off the poor Japanese man, who held his broken camera and mopped blood from his cheek with a tissue.

"He was staring at me!" She shouted, "Staring at me!"

Victor walked to the gentleman's toilet, washed his hands and face and looked deeply into the mirror.

Yes father you were right, women are trouble, Victor left the hotel for the long walk home but stopped at the first corner and looked back at the hotel. "*Hasta la vista*, baby," he yelled.

Chapter Three

DESK SERGEANT NAYLOR WAS BEING AIDED AND ABETTED BY Constable Mary Franks, trying to prepare him for the general knowledge quiz at the annual Biggar show.

"Next question Nat, which animal can survive for long periods of time without food or water and has the ability to change its skin colour to its surroundings?" Franks asked.

"I think," Naylor started, "I think it's a three toed sloth." The Constable threw the question book at Naylor.

"I've already asked you that one tonight, it's a chameleon stupid. I will make some tea."

Sergeant Bede forced his way through Stranraer Police Station's double doors drying his hair with a paper towel. At thirty-three he was shorter than most of the Strathclyde police officers, and with broad shoulders and a slightly stooped spine he carried a little more weight than his doctor had liked. He had the look of a malevolent schoolboy.

"How can a woman six feet seven inches high seem like seven feet six when she is on top of you?" Bede asked.

"On top of you?" Mary Franks asked, carrying two mugs of tea and biting on a digestive. Before he could answer Dolly burst through the doors at speed carrying a rolled up exercise mat beneath one arm, a change bag in one hand, and a small brown box in the other. She was wearing a sky blue v-neck cashmere sweater, ski pants, and long leather boots. Her blonde hair was cut attractively short.

"Give me ten minutes Bede," Dolly ordered, "and then come into my office."

Sergeant Bede was angry at the way she had spoken to him and livid that she had asked him to defuse a bomb. "Cuthbert doesn't order me around like that," he complained to Naylor.

"Don't forget George, while the Chief Inspector is away taking pictures of his deer with those old fashioned cameras, Dolly is in charge."

Ten minutes late an undeterred George Bede burst into Dolly's office. "I want a word..." Bede stopped, stunned. Dolly lay on the exercise mat doing sit ups in her light lime green t-shirt and long black tights.

"One hundred and two one hundred and three..." she counted.

Bede looked down at her pulsating long leg muscles and thought she had legs that fantasies were made of. He looked like a boxer waiting for the final bell as she speared him with her eyes.

"Bede, close the door," she ordered. "Open that hessian bag on the table and take out a booklet in there. It's for you."

He took the booklet out and read the title: *How to assemble and dismantle explosive devices.*

Bede's finger and thumb felt the soft yet robust light brown fabric of the bag.

"Looks like any other bag, Sergeant," she noted, to which Bede nodded his agreement. "Only on the KL19, the fabric is impregnated with strands of copper, oxidized copper, a highly efficient antenna. The transmitter circuitry is in the handles and the batteries are mounted in the plastic buttons on the bottom. It can transmit a signal for more than sixty miles. I designed it myself at the FBI Headquarters in Quantico Washington for a money drop."

Bede looked impressed as he opened the bag took out a damp wool hat, a leather fob holding an FBI badge, a small forensic kit and a photograph of a young Cadet dressed in a t-shirt and a Miami Dolphins baseball cap.

"That's Joe, Joe Kenna, from Key West," Dolly said, now finished her work out. "I trained him myself. He was a good agent but had one fault: he still believed in Santa Claus and thought there was good in everyone.

"He was told to take down a terrorist, to kill him, but what did he do? He wanted to take him alive. The terrorist hugged him in appreciation then blew them both up with his explosive vest. It was sad, very sad. Let that be a lesson to you Sergeant George Bede, never fall for the 'I haven't a weapon, please spare me,' routine, just shoot to kill and ask questions later."

The door opened, it was Naylor. "I don't want to spoil the party Inspector, but a call has just come in. An unexplained death reported of a young male at The Portpatrick Hotel."

"Who made the call?" Bede asked.

"It was anonymous sir, but her voice sounded like one of the street girls," Naylor answered. "I've phoned Big Sam and his Scene of Crime team and I've had the car brought around to the front for you Inspector."

"Well done Naylor," Dolly patted his shoulder, "I'm glad someone has their eyes on the job and not somewhere else personal." If looks had been weapons Bede would have been torn to shreds.

Chapter Four

BEDE AND DOLLY LEFT IN THE CORVETTE. DOLLY DROVE AND THEY were silent until they arrived at the Portpatrick Hotel car park. Big Sam Harris the pathologist was checking a clip board dressed in his full forensic outfit. His scene of crime operations team, the twin technicians Pandora and Polly Anna, were unrolling the police tape.

Bede went over to him for information while Dolly lifted the forensic suits from the boot of the car.

"Where's Big Man today?" Big Sam asked.

"Chief Inspector Cuthbert Durham is on holiday, starting from today. He's down near the Mull of Galloway taking pictures of his precious deer."

"Well it may have started today but it is also ending today. We have a suspicious death, a murder in fact. Bring him back."

"He won't be happy Sam," Bede said, rubbing his chin, "He has been looking forward to his break."

"He will be even less happy when you tell him I have just spotted an old friend of his. There's a red Jaguar two plus two parked in the car park," Sam pointed.

Big Sam Harris, Head Pathologist for Strathclyde Police, was a tall, slim and good looking man of fifty-five years. He had an excellent reputation within the force, as well as among other pathologists, and was an honorary lecturer in pathology.

He was just finishing the procedures for his initial report under a large clear plastic tent which was carried, along with a black all weather body bag, in the small trailer towed by the white van. The whole operation in the Portpatrick Hotel beer garden had been completed with military precision, professional and thorough.

While Pandora and Polly Anna started setting up a barrier of cones and tape Sam made several sketches of the body from different vantage points and at different angles. Pandora then took air and body temperature readings while her twin sister took photographs.

It was Sam who then started taking samples from beneath the victim's fingernails before placing paper bags over the hands and fastening them with rubber bands. He was meticulous in every detail; it was his way. They had conducted a hands and knees inspection of the immediate vicinity with all visits to the crime scene being timed and logged.

Sam pulled a small dictaphone from his pocket and described the crime scene, "The victim's left hand was across his chest; right hand straight down resting on the bench with his head and upper spine tilted slightly to the left."

He checked the bench but could see no drag marks. "Victim died instantaneously from the breaking of his neck, leaving noticeable spots in his eyes called petechial haemorrhages, the bursting of small blood vessels caused by pressure on the jugular. He had received a second injury, a wound to the side of the neck, caused by being stabbed with a bladed weapon, probably after his heart had stopped beating, resulting in little blood loss around the wound. Stabbing would have been at least thirty minutes after death."

Inspecting the upper spine and neck, Sam noticed the bruising and heavy marking, concluding, "A terrific amount of pressure has been applied from behind, pressing down on the spine with great force, probably by a strong male."

With no indication of a struggle or self protection from the victim, Sam hypothesised that he had been taken totally by surprise. Mercifully it would have been quick.

The victim was gently lowered into the body bag. Sam made the sign of the cross on his chest and whispered, "Bless you my son," then zipped up the bag. He was on first name terms with death, with its individual odour and its suddenness. Violent death he thought allowed the victim no dignity or privacy. Now came the part of the job Sam hated: to trace and inform loved ones.

The body was now taken away to the Glasgow mortuary, hiding unseen behind the famous law courts.

Chapter Five

CHIEF INSPECTOR CUTHBERT DURHAM'S MOOD WAS RELAXED but his intention was serious as he walked to the birdwatcher's hide on the moors. He stopped momentarily and took in the scent of the heath and heather, inhaling the essence of nature was to him like natural cocaine.

The hide consisted of a willow frame interwoven with holly and ivy, leaving two long narrow slits for viewing and allowing the sun's early morning bright rays to penetrate every inch of the hide.

He had visited the site on numerous occasions, noting the brightness of the sun at different times of the day. The light detector he used for this was new to the market, a total contrast to the camera he used. It was an early edition box Brownie, state of the art in the early nineteen twenties. He was becoming obsessed with achieving his goal: first prize in the photography competition at the Biggar show.

He had gone through the basics, checked the camera, the light meter, and distance. The stage was set: the backdrop, a short, stumpy, gnarled, wind-sculpted oak; the foreground, heather, heath, and short scrub.

He was prepared for a lengthy wait and was relaxed in his portable chair, disregarding the hard wooden benches provided by the Woodland Trust.

He sensed a change with a whisper of mist that danced like a translucent phantom to the faint chant of a gentle breeze. With his finger poised over the camera's shutter he listened. It was so quiet he could hear his own heart beat. Cuthbert was wary of his scent drifting towards his prey. Even the sound of a leaf falling was audible.

Crack, a twig snapped and Cuthbert's reactions were flung into overdrive. First a small compact fawn, playful and uncaring, then its mother, more wary, eyes peering while she sniffed the air. Eagerly he waited for the stag, the daddy of all stags.

The monarch showed, his tall proud head covered in magnificent antlers. Any second now the showman was about to make his full appearance and Cuthbert was ready with his finger poised. The monarch stopped and lifted his head high, he could detect a new scent and a sudden noise.

Cuthbert could wait; it was a game of hunter versus the hunted. His opportunity would come any second now…

"Sorry to bother you sir."

Like bone china suddenly breaking the noise was unwarranted and undoubtedly that of Detective Sergeant George Bede. Fur, feathers and leaves were sent flying and the chance was gone, the moment was lost.

"I'm on hol-li-day, Sergeant," the Chief Inspector spelled out the word while peering through one of the long narrow viewing openings.

"Not any more sir," answered a smiling George Bede.

Cuthbert could see that Bede was ruffled and on foreign ground, cut off from his comfort zone like a wild animal trapped in a cage. He knew his break was over.

Sergeant Bede carried his two cases still locked and unopened from his journey down. He had never had the time to unpack.

"Could I take a picture sir?" Bede asked, "With one of your old cameras?"

Cuthbert took the Beau Brownie from its brown leather case, "Just look down on the view finder and press the lever," he explained.

Bede took some peanuts from his starched shirt pocket and spread them onto the Bentley's emerald green bonnet. Like magic a Yellow Hammer appeared and Bede pressed the lever.

"Bingo."

Cuthbert shook his head and knew that life was sometimes slightly unbalanced. He had spent nearly a full day travelling down and setting up for the shoot and had nothing to show for it. Bede turns up and two minutes later cries bingo.

He knew some people were born brighter and more aware than others. Sometimes he thought that just once or twice a genius would be thrown up to balance things out. Cuthbert had tried and double tried to get Bede through the Strathclyde Police Force's entrance examination. One example always sprung to the Chief Inspector's thoughts, a simple question: "Name two military leaders with similar motives and humane qualities." George Bede's answer came as, "Attila the Hun and William Booth, the Salvation Army founder, as they both led armies."

"Having some work done at the back sir?" Sergeant Bede asked.

Cuthbert had gone round the back of the cottage to make a final check of windows and doors then saw them at the boundary fence. There were four of them, three local men he recognised and one much taller wearing a bright orange coat with a hood.

"Going to start some archeological dig?" Cuthbert asked.

"Anders Anderson from Sweden," the tall one announced, reaching out a huge hand. His whole body seemed huge apart from his other hand which was tiny and stiff as if taken from a small child. "People will come from miles around to see it," he smiled.

"See it?" Cuthbert queried as a huge articulated flat bed wagon pulled onto the moorland.

"I am building a new Swedish lodge made of solid Pine Timber."

"Will you not be blocking the view?" The policeman asked.

"That's why I am building it very tall," he unrolled the building plans. "The fourth story has a balcony with a viewing platform to look over the moor. You see this generator from my home country on the back of the wagon? It was designed by NASA."

He handed Cuthbert the generator's keys. Cuthbert felt the five strangely shaped keys in his hand, "Well, I suppose that with five keys you will never need to get another one cut."

"That is the whole point of the machine," Anders smiled. "No one will steal it because keys can't be cut."

"You do have planning permission for this rocket?"

"I know someone at the planning department," Anders touched the side of his nose as if to say something in code.

The Chief Inspector let Bede drive back, he felt his day had started with promise but now the promise was gone, lost in the Scottish mist.

"When is the new car coming over from America George?" He asked.

"I pick up the new Ford Explorer in the morning sir," Bede smiled. "I am the car's first owner."

Cuthbert watched the bright sun rays shine thought the tall poplars. Half asleep, he thought back to his first meeting with the young schoolboy, George Bede.

"I jis wanna be a polis, an I dinnae care whit they call me in the Drum."

Cuthbert's then Desk Sergeant Reese had complained about the young schoolboy who had called into the Stranraer station bothering him. To Cuthbert this young schoolboy was by no means a bother. He was literally a life line. Since Cuthbert's wife and son's murder he had struggled, not only to keep going but to see any real purpose in life.

"I'll take you home, young man," Cuthbert had told the young schoolboy and asked if he lived in Glasgow. The answer had been Drumchapel.

When Bede pulled the Bentley into the Glasgow mortuary car park Cuthbert turned to him.

"Before you take your exam, Sergeant, you are expected to have witnessed at least one post-mortem. Rather than pre-warn you and have you stress about it, I thought you could come in with me now and get it over with."

Bede nodded but wasn't looking forward to it. He entered the outer porch area and followed Cuthbert's instructions as they dressed in a forensic suit, over shoes, hat and face mask. Although the morgue always gave away its sinister purpose with its aroma of death, Cuthbert actually found it a cool and peaceful place.

The body was laid out on an aluminium table, naked apart from the paper bags over his hands. They crossed the tiled floor that had a sunken sluice drain in each corner.

Big Sam had already started measuring and announcing details into a small hand held tape recorder. Polly Anna was sat at a small formica table taking notes for Sam's own file.

Pandora helped Sam with the menial tasks, placing the body block under the neck, removing the paper bags from the hands, and taking skin samples from beneath the fingernails and hands. A large Y-marking had been drawn on the torso from the chest area down to the abdomen, a guide to where the cut would be made.

Sam and Polly Anna stood back as Pandora started taking photographs. It was co-ordinated and methodical, or as Bede suggested later, "Like three butchers carving up a Christmas turkey."

Cuthbert joined Big Sam in an outer room. He was running a small vacuum pipe over the victim's clothing, which was spread out on a long bench. Long strips of tape were then pressed onto the cloth and removed. Everything would be labelled, bagged and sent upstairs to the particulates lab.

"Who is the tall chap we passed on the way in Sam, he was tall and thin and looked like death?" Cuthbert asked?

"Lurch, the exhibits officer. He brought this complaint form in about the girls, they tease him but it's just a bit of fun to lighten the atmosphere. When he started he didn't know there were two of them, being twins, well you can imagine." Sam smiled as he put the complaint form into the pedal bin. The girls had taped the word "complaints" onto the pedal of the bin.

"Where's George?" Big Sam asked.

"It's his first autopsy, so he may be freshening up in the toilet,"

Cuthbert told him. "You must have seen some bodies in your time, I wonder if you ever have dreams?" Cuthbert asked.

"Nightmares, you mean," Sam replied. "The first case I ever took charge of was a young girl with deep blue eyes. For two or three weeks I kept seeing those eyes and I couldn't sleep, so I vowed that I would never again look into a person's eyes. The eyes are the soul of the body."

"Sometimes, when I first arrive at a murder scene, I purposely look into the victim's eyes. The silent witness relays to me in a series of flashing lights and I see the perpetrator, not clear but the outline, and then I just fall to the floor," Cuthbert told him.

Bede came in looking as white as a ghost.

"Let's get you home George and call it a day," Cuthbert said, "You've got your post-mortem over and out of the way."

Big Sam grabbed Cuthbert by the sleeve, "Before you go, I wanted to say: Pandora's been over to Canada on one of these student exchange programmes. Now she's thinking of emigrating and going to a college in Charlotte near Quebec. She's studying French in Glasgow, night classes, everything in Quebec is in English and French. She has met this chap called Pierre Fontaines, he's a good deal older than us. Since she's come back nothing seems the same."

"You worried about being short handed?" Cuthbert asked.

"It's not so much that, it is more the fact that since she has come back she's been goading Polly Anna in French, her having a boyfriend and her twin sister never having one."

Sam shook his head as Pandora came in for the plunger.

"Things will get back to normal Sam," Cuthbert answered, "Just give her time to dream." "Yesterday after the girls had their sandwiches she said to Polly Anna *allons-y trou du cul*, and had a big grin on her face."

"Bon jour, comment ça va?" Pandora asked Cuthbert.

"Bien bien. Une ventouse?" Cuthbert said in reply.

"Oui, oui," she smiled, lifting the plunger and leaving.

"You speak French?" Sam asked.

"A bit, I went to Paris with Margaret and Kelvin to take in the sights and we went to a Marc Riboud Exhibition, he's a top photographer, mainly deeply atmospheric images of mountains and forests covered in mist. Sam," he went on, "you need not worry about Pandora, things will come right again. And by the way, what she said was 'let's roll arsehole' to Polly Anna. It's called changes Sam, she is growing up."

As Cuthbert opened his Bentley door he noticed Polly Anna standing beside the perimeter chain link fence. "You alright Polly Anna?" he asked. "Have you been crying?" She ran to Cuthbert and hugged him, just as she had done as a child. He had known the girls and their mother, a heroin addict who took one hit too many. He had raised them, paying their university fees and being there for them like a father.

"Uncle Cuthbert," Polly Anna sobbed, "Nothing's the same. I used to know Pandora, we could read each other's minds, but now she's pulled the plug, I can't contact her, I don't understand her and to top it all she says nasty things in French. I hate these changes."

"How do you know the things Pandora says are insults?" Cuthbert asked, "If the words are in French?"

"I know Pandora," Polly Anna replied, "and I know that laugh."

"Why don't I take you somewhere nice some night, like I used to? I'll bring a book with French phrases in it and you can get your own back on your twin sister and say things she doesn't know."

"I'd like that Uncle Cuthbert," Polly Anna answered. "I miss the old times." As she lay in his arms Cuthbert thought back to the changes he had made in his own life, many changes. He decided he needed time to think and so, after saying goodbye to Polly Anna, he made his way back down to his holiday cottage to get an early night.

He was woken by loud banging on his front door. It was Eric, Eric the Viking, holding two clear plastic bags. A small cardboard box was at his feet. He was Cuthbert's closest neighbour and yet lived a full mile away in the Old Coaching House. He was unshaven, had alert eyes like a hawk, and stood close to seven feet tall, more like a giant than a Viking.

"Grandchildren staying," he said, handing Cuthbert the two clear plastic bags. "Keep them separate," he instructed as he sauntered off.

Cuthbert brought the small cardboard box holding fish food and a booklet on keeping catfish inside. *So*, Cuthbert thought, *his grandchildren turning up means he'll have to fill in the ponds, for safety reasons.*

He held up the first bag containing Sammy Davis. *Likes half an orange once a week*, Eric had written on it, but when he held up the bag the catfish made for his face.

"Yes, I'll keep you apart alright."

When he picked up the second bag holding Eartha Kitt she came to the top of the bag and again he read the tag, *she likes the sound of soft guitar music*. Cuthbert smiled as he didn't realise that they could hear. Or was it one of the Viking's little jokes? He dressed and put the catfish into the two separate ponds. Sammy went in the bigger lower pond and Eartha into the higher feeder tank as it held the fountain.

He flicked on the fountain and brought out his guitar and began to play. Instantly Eartha started to move up and down in the water as if dancing and then lay on her back. Cuthbert leaned down and was close to the water when he stroked her. She responded with a special show, swimming in and out of the little castle and over the drawbridge. Cuthbert looked down on Sammy but he was not happy, in fact he was angrier.

During the night Cuthbert was woken by the sound of thrashing. When he opened the bedroom window he saw Sammy was in Eartha's pond, chasing her. He raced outside carrying his long fishing net but was surprised to see that all was well and both were in there own separate ponds.

"Well I never," he whispered to himself and suddenly saw Eartha came up to the surface.

"Yes Eartha, life is not easy," She stared at him then swam to the darker lower edge under the footbridge and looked down at Sammy.

"I hope you are not a bully Sammy," Cuthbert said, throwing him half an orange that he quickly started to nibble at.

Cuthbert pulled back one of the fence panels and walked across to the huge generator, which stood like a Trojan horse on the skyline. He pulled the keys from the starter and went back to bed.

Chapter Six

BACK IN STRANRAER POLICE STATION NAYLOR AND FRANKS WERE again busy with questions and answers for the Biggar show.

"Here's a question Sergeant," the Chief Inspector said as he entered the station. "Two kestrels on a hen house roof and the farmer shoots and kills one of them. The question is, how many kestrels are left on the roof?"

"Can we think on that sir?" Mary Franks asked.

"Yes," replied Cuthbert, "but there is more than one answer."

"Two phone calls came in first thing sir," Naylor announced. "A small white van arrived at the Stranraer Ferry Terminal. It had been booked for last night's sailing from Belfast but was unclaimed when it docked. It has been put in the long stay car park."

"Wonder if it has anything to do with this murder. Has anyone reported a missing person yet?" Cuthbert asked.

"Not yet sir," Naylor replied, "but the victim is known locally as Patrick Dolan from Port Stewart."

"Big Paddy? That's Seamus O' Connell's cousin, and he probably doesn't even know yet," Cuthbert said. "What about time of death, and who reported finding the body?"

"Anonymous sir, sounded like a street girl, then a young barmaid walked in off the street," Naylor went on reading from the report sheet, *I stuck him with the broken glass because he was staring at me.* The time of statement was ten thirty-three, she's with Constable Jolly now sir and she's made her some tea. She gave her name as Jinty, Jinty Ferguson sir."

A spark lit up in Cuthbert's eyes; it was a name from the past. "What was the other phone call Sergeant?" He asked.

"Home Office official memorandum has been sent to you about a Commander Hamilton staying at the Portpatrick Hotel on official business."

Cuthbert nodded, *so that's Big Sam's face from the past*, he thought.

"That Jinty Ferguson sir, she seems to be in another world," Naylor worried.

"Make sure she is always accompanied Sergeant, preferably by a female officer. We had one of these last year, a young chap saying he had just killed someone and it turned out he was in a secure unit at the time," Cuthbert frowned, "receiving treatment."

Sergeant George Bede pulled the Ford Explorer into the Stranraer Police Station's car park and glanced down at the mileage indicator, thirty-three miles it read. *This monster will turn some heads* he thought *and will cause some fireworks.*

That's when he saw something bounce and then roll under the new car. He got out and crouched down, looking beneath. All he saw was white light accompanied by a huge boom.

When Bede woke the following morning he gazed around the hospital room and felt warmed by the pale yellow walls and the silver shadows from the window blinds. He tried to make out the faces looking down at him but could hear nothing. He was too drugged up to pay much attention to the burning sensation over every inch of his face.

"You are in hospital George," Cuthbert mouthed. The Doctor had said Bede's hearing may be temporarily impaired but that overall he was satisfactory. *Satisfactory to whom?* Cuthbert had thought.

Bede looked like he had put his head into a bonfire and his singed ears were curled up like a fortune cookie. The hair he had left on his head looked like gunpowder, black and lifeless, and his whole face looked like a barbecued mole. His wife Lisa looked terrified and his son Jonathon looked down on him like a termite.

"You are going to be alright," Lisa now mouthed, "you just need some rest."

Bede started to get agitated and his eyes started to blink rapidly. He put his hands out in front of him as if he was holding a steering wheel and then started pointing to himself.

"Your car is a right off George," Cuthbert explained. "It took the full blast. It was blown into the air and unfortunately landed on the new police van. You were saying earlier when you were being loaded into the ambulance about it rolling under the car George, what was it?" Bede made a fist with his bald hand and lifted his little finger like a pin. With his other hand he mimicked pulling out the pin and then began to shake violently, reliving the experience.

"Gently George, gently. Are you saying it was a hand grenade?" Lisa asked and he started nodding.

Chapter Seven

CUTHBERT JOINED JOLLY IN THE INTERVIEW ROOM. JOLLY WAS A numbingly bright girl in her early twenties with an expression of jollity she wore like a Halloween mask, slightly over weight with short chubby legs, a short fringe and no makeup or jewellery.

"Jinty Ferguson," Cuthbert started, "you say this chap had been in the bar on the Friday night and earlier. Had anyone made a threat against him?"

"He came in on the Thursday," she replied, "in the early evening. He looked like he'd had a few drinks and as soon as he came in he starts with his eyes, staring, he didn't say anything but I knew, even with my back to him, he was staring at me, then an hour later these two from the factory, foreigners, both dark skinned, I hear loud voices, arguing like, and the table goes over. This Irishman and a smaller one were rolling on the floor and having a go at each other."

"You don't know what it was about then? Was there anyone else in the bar?" Jolly asked.

"Don't know what it was about, there was Sally Harris behind the bar with me and just the Irishman and those two, oh and yes an old chap in a suit, a gentleman I think. They seemed to know him."

Hamilton, Cuthbert wrote down, *Commander Hamilton and he is no gentleman.*

"On the Friday, Jinty, did the two foreign men come in to the bar?" Again it was Jolly doing the questioning.

"No, they only came during the week, they travelled back home at weekends."

"Now you say he was staring on the Thursday, this Irishman, was he staring on the Friday?"

"Yes, yes, even worse, he was, again he never said much, in fact he gave me a compliment but I knew he was staring and I watched him go outside to sit in the sunshine in the Japanese garden. I went outside about half an hour later to bring in empties and noticed he was still there but looked different."

"In what way did he look different Jinty?"

"His body was leaning to one side, like he was listening to a radio or something, and I noticed this broken Champagne glass in the bin, shaped like a knife, it was. I thought now's my chance and I went up behind him and pushed it in, twisting it."

"He didn't turn to meet you or say anything or look surprised?"

"Just sat like a dummy, he never answered, like he was asleep or fainted."

"Or dead," Cuthbert jumped in, "Maybe someone had got to him before you. Did you see anyone else in the garden that night?"

She shook her head.

"For the tape Jinty," the Constable prompted.

"No miss, I saw no one," she answered.

"One last thing Jinty, that mark beneath your eye, was that caused on Friday?" Cuthbert asked

"No sir," she answered, "that's just a birthmark. I came straight in and owned up. I did the right thing, always own up I do."

Jolly led Jinty Ferguson back to the cells. Cuthbert was pleased with the way she had shown good interviewing skills, and thought the experience would do her good. She was a young constable with a very promising future.

Cuthbert went to the Bentley, turned the radio off and his anxiety on. He knew this would be an intricate and complex case.

Chapter Eight

AS CUTHBERT ENTERED THE HOSPITAL'S GAMES ROOM HE WAS met by the sound of Sergeant Bede's booming laugh.

"Your voice coming back George?"

"Still a bit sore," Bede laid the snooker cue down on the table and rubbed his hand against his throat.

"He needs more rest I am telling him," his snooker opponent, Doctor Patel, said.

"Step outside for one moment Sergeant, I have something to show you."

As George Bede stepped through the fire exit his eyes and mouth lit up.

"The garage says their insurance will cover the cost of the Explorer and wondered if this one would replace it."

Bede felt along the car's bonnet. "A Ford Thunderbird, the T Bird," Bede whispered, "voted the nineteen fifty-eight luxury car of the year."

"With three hundred and fifty horsepower. Just feel those circular headlamps."

Bede sat behind the wheel and started the engine.

"Where do you think you are going Mr George?" Doctor Patel asked.

"Those big headlamps got me thinking, I have to see Lisa."

"When will you be coming back George?" Cuthbert asked.

"I am going somewhere I have never been before," Bede laughed, "I will see you in the morning."

Chapter Nine

BEDE WAS ALREADY AT THE PORTPATRICK HOTEL WHEN Cuthbert arrived. He had been instructed to work with Inspector Malone in setting up tables, chairs and a small buffet to feed the additional troops drafted in to do house to house calls in the village concerning Patrick Dolan's murder.

As he watched his Sergeant tucking into hot pasties and washing them down with chilled beer, Cuthbert wondered what planet Bede was on. What made his blood boil more than anything was the fact he was sitting in the same seat in the Japanese garden that poor Paddy had been murdered in.

"Nice set up here sir," Bede said, struggling to talk with his mouth full of corned beef. "Food and beer on tap Pity we couldn't drag this out a bit."

"Sergeant, I have just had to inform Patrick Dolan's parents that poor Paddy won't be coming home and they want answers."

"Sorry sir, I suppose I did sound a bit heartless," Bede wiped his mouth on the paper napkin and unfastened his belt.

"Notice anything strange about that seat you're sitting in George?"

Bede shook his head and looked underneath.

"That tape with the words on, did you not notice it?"

Bede stood up, horrified. "Jesus, I never noticed, it must be where Paddy was murdered." He slowly read the words to himself, *Murder Scene Do not Cross.*

"Do you know where Inspector Malone is?" Cuthbert asked.

"Yes, she came out when I arrived and said she would be in the dining hall setting up if I needed her."

"What was the task were you given George, when you were told to report here this morning?" Cuthbert continued.

"Ah yes, I had better get down there now," Bede said hurriedly, nearly tripping over the black and yellow tape.

As Cuthbert looked over the murder scene two gardeners approached from the back of the hotel. They could easily have been father and son.

"I don't want you to work near the murder scene here," Cuthbert explained, pointing and waving his arms. The older of the two said what work they had been assigned to do, pointing to a bed of thick stalked red bamboo, but Cuthbert could make no sense of anything he said. All his words coiled the vowels together. They may as well have been aliens, for they certainly were not locals.

Cuthbert was amazed how quickly Dolly had transformed the dining room into an active HQ for the investigation. One corner had been screened off with filing cabinets to form an office area with telephones ready for action. A central area beside a hand washbasin was used to house two trestle tables capable of holding a water boiler and a coffee percolator with all manner of cups and side plates.

"Just admiring your handy work Dolly, I am very impressed. What's on the other side of the cabinets?" Cuthbert asked.

"Come around and I will show you," Dolly led the way to a bank of monitor screens. "There is good news and bad as far as the hotels CCTV cameras are concerned. The good news is every road and footpath is covered by a camera."

"So no person could come or go without being recorded? No blind spots?" Cuthbert asked.

"Now that's the bad news," Dolly spread out a plan of the Japanese garden. "Here and here," she pointed, "are beds of red bamboo. You know that bamboo is the fastest growing plant known to man?"

"So we have active cameras everywhere other than the one place we needed a camera," Cuthbert asked and Dolly nodded. "Where's Bede at now? He was supposed to be helping you."

"I gave him a good dressing down and he started to sulk so I sent him to the kitchen to get the water boiler sorted."

"The two gardeners, I met them earlier. Were they here on Friday?" Cuthbert enquired.

"No, they just came up from Manham in Norfolk this morning. I want the bamboo cutting right back. Something may have been thrown or hidden in there as it's so close to the murder scene. I couldn't get anyone local to do it," Dolly explained.

"That explains the accents," Cuthbert smiled.

As Cuthbert entered the kitchen he found a girl struggling with a large basket of cutlery.

"Let me help you with that," he said, rushing over to grab it and set it down on the drainer. "Could you not see she was struggling, George?"

"She never asked for help sir," Bede replied, again struggling to speak with his mouth full.

"You look tired and over worked," Cuthbert turned his attention back to the girl, "I'm Cuthbert Durham, responsible for all of this chaos."

"I know," she answered, "I'm Sally Harris, kitchen porter, barmaid, parlour maid, you name it."

"Why not let me get you a cup of tea and take the weight off your feet?" he asked.

"It is hard work sir, hotel work," she said. Sally was more attractive than pretty and had her hair tied up in a barrette.

"A friend of yours?" Cuthbert nodded to the young man sitting in the kitchen area wearing a pin striped suit, holding a clip board and looking at his watch.

"He is from the Health and Safety brigade. I had to get the metal railings taken down at the side in case a child falls from the sky and lands on the railings. Then last week some lad complained about getting black paint on his trousers. Now he says they must be 'removed from the site forthwith.'" Sally mimicked his voice and they both laughed.

"Were you in the bar Friday night, Sally?"

"Yes," she answered pouring two cups of tea, "as was Jinty Ferguson, the relief girl. The Vietnamese girl Diep was on reception."

"Jinty wasn't herself and said someone had been staring at her early on. I told her to be careful, what with her being on a final warning over a similar incident with a guest last month. She scratched his face something awful."

"You say she scratched his face, but did she put her hands near his neck or around his neck?" he asked.

"No, it happened so quickly. I would have struggled to pull her off him but her boyfriend lifted her off one handed," Sally answered.

"So she has a boyfriend who is tall and strong?" Cuthbert asked.

"Yes, could have been a body builder." Sally thought back, "His name is in the reservations book as he ordered two meals."

"Think back, could he have been staying here in the hotel and come down, maybe through the kitchen, and gone out through these French doors straight into the Japanese garden?" He asked.

"It's possible, it's Diep who deals with the hotel bookings. I can get that name for you tonight."

"Is Jinty a local girl Sally?" Cuthbert asked.

"No, Glasgow or Paisley," Sally thought, "but not local."

"One last thing," the Chief Inspector asked, "is a chap called Hamilton staying at the hotel? He'd be elderly, wears a suit and drives a Jaguar car."

"Yes I know him," she answered. "He's on the top floor, the attic room. I have noticed he goes down to the beach after high tide every day looking for pebbles or shells."

Or a body, Cuthbert thought, knowing Hamilton was trouble.

"He's in the bar at the moment," she told him.

Hamilton stood out like a Dolphin's fin on a calm blue sea, with his dark blue suit and dark hair going grey at the sides. He was reading a boating magazine as Cuthbert walked from the bar.

"Commander Hamilton, on my patch and not so much as a note on my desk." Cuthbert spat.

"Well Durham," Hamilton answered, losing interest in his magazine. "I wondered when you would show up. I'm on holiday, beach combing for shells and pebbles."

"I know you Hamilton, where you go trouble follows. I just hope those aren't live shells. Take note, if you so much as wear a loud jumper in public I will have you. Before you start to scratch I want to know when you felt the itch."

Hamilton smiled and then went back to his reading.

Cuthbert returned to the dining room and noticed Bede finally helping Dolly with the last of the preparations, emptying storage boxes filled with box files, pin boards, action forms, forensic submission forms, questionnaires and maps of the area. Slowly the extra officers started filing in, stretching their legs after the bus journey down from Glasgow. They made for the teas and coffees then the buffet.

His main operations team were hungry, both for something to eat and for information, looking for some sort of an indication as to which way the operation was to be tackled. Dolly came over to Cuthbert, looking confused.

"I wonder why a girl with natural blonde hair would put black hair dye on her roots to make herself look like a bottle-blonde?" She nodded to indicate which girl.

"Barbie Campbell Mackenzie," Cuthbert whispered, reading from the roster, "I think we should watch her."

Cuthbert clapped his hands together and silence did not so much fall as land.

"Firstly I want every single person here to realise that they are an important and invaluable part of this team. Clear and concise logging of all interviews and door to door enquiries are a must. The most important factor in the murder enquiry is time, and time has been lost so now we play catch up. Inspector Malone has made up a pack for you. It contains an outline of the inquiry, a questionnaire to be fully filled in and signed, and lastly a map of the area.

"You will go out in pairs within two groups. The first group will be on foot; you will cover houses, pubs, shops and the local fishermen. I have spoken to the Harbour Master, Captain Jack at the old light house, and he knows more than anyone about the comings and goings of sea farers.

"Now the second group will cover the isolated cottages, small holdings, farms and the like. Have a word with Sergeant Bede as he has the rota for transport arrangements. At the end of your shifts please give your completed packs to Inspector Malone, the Administration Operations Manager."

"Can I point out here," Dolly interrupted, "if you are unable to contact someone that day, log the missed call and make that call a priority the next day. That one missed call just might hold vital information."

"Thank you Inspector," Cuthbert took control again, "I want you all to think of the operation in terms of Dos and Don'ts. All reports and logging must be clear and accurate with no sloppy reporting. Don't antagonise the local people, the people of Portpatrick are proud, hard working, and they fear there still might be a killer in the village. Any questions?"

Constable Franks poked a very small finger skywards.

"Yes Constable Franks?"

"If the team on the ground gets a bit of stick about the delay in getting started and the locals have heard about this barmaid's confession, what should our stance be?"

"Well, that is a good question Mary. Sometimes unfortunately we have to play things by the book. The body has not formally been identified and so our course of action is in accordance with laid down police procedures. I know many of you will be thinking that the bar maid has confessed to stabbing the victim, but can I make this absolutely clear: please don't taint your resolve on this inquiry with any prejudice. If someone confesses to a crime and later retracts that confession, or say a local lunatic asylum tells us they were guests at their establishment at the time of the incident, then it leaves the enquiry in a mess. So let's get moving and, again, my thanks go to each and every one of you. Don't forget that food and drink have been laid on, so tuck in."

"Over the bloody top! Never mind feeding them, I would have got them working," Sergeant Bede snarled at Mary Franks.

"George, he's got the team motivated, fed and watered. He will probably keep them going till ten o' clock tonight. Cuthbert's no fool, so just have a pasty and remember, George, you've a lot to learn from him."

Bede bit his lip and sighed, "I don't think I will bother with a pasty, I feel a bit bloated."

Chapter Ten

WHEN CUTHBERT ENTERED STRANRAER POLICE STATION'S double doors he heard a sound like the repetitive beat of an Amazonian drummer. Desk Sergeant Naylor was smiling while reading a comic.

"Have you been thinking about the kestrel on the hen house roof Nat?" Cuthbert asked.

"Well, it was more of Mary Franks thinking than mine," Naylor answered, "but she thought the hen house roof might not be pitched or only slightly sloping and so the Kestrel, although dead, might still be on the roof as it had not rolled off."

"Good answer Naylor, ten out of ten. That's half the puzzle solved," the Chief Inspector answered.

"Inspector Mole is in your office sir," Naylor informed him. "A flying visit on behalf of the Chief in Glasgow, he says he's doing voluntary hospital radio now."

"It's alright Naylor," Cuthbert said, "I can hear who is in there. He's brought his cronies with him."

Cuthbert stood outside his door for a moment and listened: "The problem with Durham is he tries to understand the criminals, the prostitutes and other riff raff, He tries to be a social worker, not a Chief Inspector. He sympathises with them."

Inspector Mole's face changed colour like a piece of litmus paper, from bright red to grey, when the Chief Inspector entered his office.

"Cuthbert... I thought you were away taking your photographs."

"Stand when you talk to me Mole, and address me as sir," Cuthbert was furious. "One thing I pride myself on Inspector is the fact I never get angry. But this time I have failed. I train, I spar and I box to gain respect for myself and my opponents." He picked Mole up by the collar, leaving his feet dangling above the ground. "I've been told on good authority, Mole, that when you die you will only have one handle on your coffin, and that will be on the inside, so get yourself back to your friend Antonio Vetch in Glasgow."

Mole moved like the last passenger leaving a sinking liner.

"Mole," the Chief Inspector continued, "I hear you do requests on the radio. Well my request is that you close the door on the way out."

Chapter Eleven

IT HAD BEEN A LONG DAY BUT CUTHBERT HAD MADE GOOD TIME driving back to his cottage at Kemin Bay. As he turned a sharp corner he came up behind a long low loader carrying huge wooden frames. They were so tall they were catching the overhead branches of trees.

Anders Anderson, Cuthbert thought, *and his pine white elephant.*

Suddenly something dark slapped against the Bentley's windscreen and Cuthbert pulled into the side of the road. He saw it was a raven, not the whole bird just the head and tail feathers. The poor bird must have flown into the wooden panels and been decapitated.

Once home he wrapped it in some tissue and placed it in a small wooden box, adorning it with some sea shells and pebbles he found around the fountain. He sat out in the long shadow beside his two ponds. Even the catfish Sammy Davis and Eartha Kitt seemed edgy watching the large wooden edifice push up from out of the ground like a giant mushroom eating away the sunlight. It was starting to dwarf the cottage and it was only half way up.

He knew he wouldn't sleep due to the noise of the generator

Anders had brought in and the brightness of the mega watt security arc lights. He'd had enough, the lights now were flickering and the generator was making a high pitched whirring sound. As he caught his own reflection in a mirror it looked like he was watching an old black and white film.

He crept down to the back fence, slipped between the fence panels and stood beside the generator. He unscrewed the petrol tank filler cap and emptied his kidneys straight in.

The flickering became even more evident and the whirling got even louder and then suddenly the generator exploded sending oil and metal flying. He then climbed the wide wooden chalet staircase and laid the wooden box on the floor of one of the upper rooms, noticing the moonlight shining from the dead raven's eye.

Chapter Twelve

DOLLY HAD ALREADY STARTED UNLOADING THE SMALL WHITE van when Bede pulled up. "I've dismantled the wooden crate and have made a start," she announced. "Ferry Master says two factory owners have been hanging around the van, one was an Arab and the other a Somali."

"I've run a check on the van's number plate; it comes up as a Honda moped owned by a girl in Larne," Bede replied.

"I'll pass every item to you Bede, I'll name it while you log it and I'll bag it," Dolly said, and Bede nodded.

"One bullet proof jacket, Colt mark twenty six three thirty eight special, double action revolver, one box of nine millimetre parabellum ammunition armour piercing, one Glock seventeen, one Glock nineteen specially modified, one box of soft nosed nine mm parabellums, one military ka-bar knife blade coated in black epoxy, one Uzi, one Glock ten, one carton of sound suppressors hand packed with mineral cotton wadding, one Colt Python, one Smith and Wesson thirty three, one box of twelve gauge shock lock rounds and finally one box of long range hardnosed rifle bullets."

"Enough to arm a regiment," Bede concluded.

"Yes," Dolly answered, "but more likely to be what we would call a travelling salesman's bag, full of what the world's buyers want, as in the case of a hit and run unit of about ten men, plenty of arms but little ammunition."

Chapter Thirteen

IT WAS MID-MORNING WHEN THE CHIEF INSPECTOR ENTERED THE small Portpatrick corner shop. Margo Franks was clearing away the breakfast things readying the small café section for lunches.

"You've brought the sunshine with you Cuthbert," Margo announced, "and how's our Mary doing?"

"I'm very pleased with her," Cuthbert replied, "I think she could do very well for herself. It was Mary I wanted to talk to you about Margo. Old Sandy, the retired Harbour Master from up beside the old light house, has died so we are one short for the Biggar show judging team. Do you think that Mary could fill in? I know it's short notice, but I think she's up to it."

"Well Cuthbert," Margo answered, "Mary sets the questions for a good few local pub quiz teams so I could put it to her tonight and see what she thinks."

"How's your cake coming along for the Biggar show Margo? You've never won it yet," he asked.

Margo Franks was shorter than most in the village, with golden eyes and short dark hair greying at the sides. She wore expensive blue jeans and a cranberry red turtle neck sweater and cowboy boots. "Well Cuthbert, believe it or not I had a congregation down from Dundee offering a few tips and a secret ingredient. As they have always won the trophy I thought I would give it a try." She passed Cuthbert one of her home made pasties on a white paper plate.

He walked along the harbour and found the pasty was hot and delicious. It was then he noticed a man he thought he knew, tall, emaciated and very gaunt with a look of death about him. He had a face like a handful of bones, eyes fixed in a hypnotic stare, like the stare of a dying pilgrim. His fine white long hair, silk like and unkempt came down to his shoulders. His long, black, dirty, buttonless coat stretched down to his ankles and just covered his grim threadbare deck shoes. His toe nails could be seen through the cloth. He had been Margaret's father, Ahab, Cuthbert's father in law. The loss of his daughter and grandson, blown up on the Portpatrick Belle, had turned him into this, an apprentice cadaver.

Cuthbert climbed the steep bank up towards the Portpatrick Hotel and golf course and entered Flora MacDonald's garden. He spied Flora, Margaret's mother, on a fold away chair beside a large canvas resting on a wooden easel, paints and brushes in front of her.

Grief had also aged her and deep worry lines etched her forehead. She wore a tight ponytail on her greying hair revealing her small sticky out ears. Her black and white collie, Ralf, rushed to greet him, licking his outstretched hand.

Flora wore little jewellery, two ear studs and a small silver crucifix. She was painting a portrait of the Portpatrick Belle, her daughter's boat.

"I've been told it's finished but every day I find a fault and make an improvement," Flora said, "it gets addictive."

"Maybe you don't want it to be finished Flora," Cuthbert said.

"In some way Margaret and Kelvin are still with you. It is two years today."

"Yes you needn't remind me," Flora answered, pointing to a garland on a side table. "Grief takes you to a dark lonely place, a desperate place, but it also exposes inner strengths and talents you didn't know existed. It might be we both need not only time but an understanding of why someone would do this to them."

Cuthbert shook his head, "I only wish it had been me and not them. Sometimes I blame myself."

"It is so unfair," Flora continued, pouring boiling water into a silver tea pot. "Just look at poor Ahab, down at the harbour, swears he's seen Kelvin's face in the water," she said.

"At first I thought the bomb was meant for me and I just wanted to pack in and give it up, life and the job, everything."

"Margaret would not have wanted that, she would have wanted you to do your duty Cuthbert," Flora replied.

"Duty…" Cuthbert paused, "It was my duty that got Margaret and Kelvin killed."

Cuthbert walked back down the steep hill from Flora's garden to the sea wall. The water lapping against the harbour wall and the smell of the flowers and blossom had made him feel different. The pollen he inhaled through his nostrils landed like ecstasy.

He noticed the sound of his feet changing from the dust dry boards to the deep moist sand. There was one yacht sailing out in the bay fighting the strong breeze under the clouds and a small blue painted pleasure boat tied up near the beach, The King Billy.

Both brothers were busy beside the blue gleaming boat. Seamus the elder brother was washing down the deck with a mop while his brother Sean was blowing air into one of two giant arm bands.

He took off his shirt revealing a tattoo on his arm of a dancing girl in a grass skirt. Every time he flexed his muscle she danced.

"Seamus, it's important I ask you something," Cuthbert said. "Is Paddy over on one of his runs with his van?"

"He has been, but he'll be back now as it's been over a week."

"You haven't been back home then, back to Larne. You've not heard?"

"Heard Cuthbert?" now Sean came over and joined them.

"A murder at the hotel on Friday night Sean, we think it might be Paddy. You've not spoken to him or any of his family then?"

"Paddy's like the wind, he comes and goes," Sean said.

Cuthbert pulled a large bottle of Arran Special from his coat pocket. "I hope I'm wrong, but did his white van have Irish plates?" he asked.

"Oh Irish all right, just like Paddy," Seamus answered.

"Paddy could have a fight whenever he wanted," Sean said, "and even when he didn't."

"Yes and he liked the girls," Seamus added.

"Paddy, he will be missed," Cuthbert drank to his health. "I'll take you up to Glasgow Seamus in the morning, just to check."

Cuthbert made his way back to the hotel HQ, where Dolly was going through the early questionnaires while Bede stacked the tables and chairs.

"How's it going Dolly, any problems?"

"Only one," she answered. "The teams working in the village are doing well except with one cottage, The Rook. No answer on three occasions."

"That's McDuff," Cuthbert confirmed. "They call him the Bird Man."

"More like the Knickers Man sir," Bede could not resist the urge for humour, "He always wins the photography prize with his birds though."

"Yes all right Bede," Cuthbert tried to settle the overjoyed Sergeant. "McDuff served his probation for theft from residents' washing lines and we don't want any silly interferences hampering the inquiry. I'll go around and talk to McDuff myself, Dolly.

"The magistrate turned down my request to search the factory in Well Road, so I was wondering if you two could drive past there tonight," Cuthbert suggested.

"You want us to break in sir?" Bede asked.

"Have you any other questions Sergeant?" Cuthbert went on, "The factory is on Well Road Industrial Estate, the old treacle works. It's leased to a Russian company called Valspar making nuts, bolts, brackets and hinges. The Arab and Somali run it. We need to get in the factory and see if there is a link to the weapons in the van or to Hamilton."

"Do you want us to break in sir?" Bede again asked.

"Do you want to ask another question Sergeant?"

"Can we have the night off sir?" Dolly asked,

"Yes," Cuthbert answered, "it's an old building so be careful. And you two don't get caught."

While Cuthbert was on his way to McDuff's cottage just across from the hotel he noticed Sally, the hotel worker, sitting on a low wall behind the kitchen area.

"Can I join you Sally?" Cuthbert asked, "It's nice to see the sunshine."

"Take a seat Cuthbert," she answered, "I have that name for you: Swan, Victor Swan. I am taking the afternoon off to see my granddad Blackie, Blackie Harris. He lives on the Old Mill Road."

"You mean the chess player Blackie Harris?" Cuthbert quizzed, "But that's Big Sam's father isn't it?"

"Yes, Big Sam used to be my father," Sally answered. "I know that sounds strange but he had big ideas for me when I was a young girl. He wanted me to follow him into the pathology field but for one thing I could not stand the sight of blood, and then I fell pregnant with Raymond. Funnily enough Raymond is forever reading books on bones, blood and all that stuff."

"Well…" Cuthbert wondered, "I never connected you with Sam and your dad. Mill Road is handy for the boxing club, I train myself at the Old Mill Club. Is your dad not into boxing?"

"No not boxing, chess and poker. Blackie is a chess master and played all over the world. He played and beat Garry Kasparov."

"Would you like a lift Sally? I would like to meet this chess master, he just might give me an insight on solving this murder."

Bede drove the Ford Thunderbird the short distance to the factory with Dolly; they said nothing, a dialogue of uneasiness.

"You will not be used to travelling in style Dolly, just having the Ferrari Italia." Bede commented.

"Ever heard of the Lincoln town car Sergeant?" Dolly asked, "When I was training the American network in hand writing codes at the FBI Quantico I drove a Lincoln, top of the range V8 engine, 289 horsepower, electronic traction control, automatic rear suspension, levelling, facility. Comfort and speed in one car."

Bede's ego had just deflated like a punctured balloon. "To get that passenger door open you have to bang on the door at the bottom," he crumpled.

Pulling up outside Blackie's house Cuthbert sat and admired the views out to sea. A ferry had just docked and streams of trucks and cars were abandoning the boat.

"Be patient with Granddad Cuthbert," Sally said. "He is at a funny age and doesn't see many visitors."

They moved into the house, "Granddad, look who I've brought to see you," Sally shouted, "He's a bit deaf, you have to raise your voice."

"She's told me about you," Blackie shouted.

"She tells me you used to play chess and poker Blackie," Cuthbert noted Sally pointed to the kitchen and made a T impression with her fingers.

"Yes, chess, now that's a thing," Blackie answered. "It has been a long time. You know what the secret to a good master is? It's to create an image, an impression such that your opponent thinks he can read you, then like the venetian fly trap you close the trap, snap shut."

"Granddad, don't be so melodramatic, you'll frighten him off," Sally said.

Cuthbert found the room was well furnished but untidy with abandoned clothes over chairs and discarded newspapers on a table. Blackie was a man for whom housework was a women's task; the line was not to be crossed. He had a long carved face, a long parrot shaped nose with huge staring eyes and fine silver hair. Peering over his spectacles he looked positively biblical and lighting his large briar pipe reminded Cuthbert of the burning bush.

The room had an air of time about it, with a lovely Italian clock on the sideboard, a bronze lion either side of a dial, a grandfather ticking in the hall way, and an expensive Swiss square clock on the mantle. With so many clocks Cuthbert wondered whether he was holding on to time or pushing it on.

"How do you convince your opponent that you are readable and vulnerable to him?" Cuthbert asked.

"It is a case of casting a false image, a false impression to your opponent. I make out I have made a mistake and I am guilty and open about it, then the opponent takes advantage, takes full control and by human nature feels dominant over his opponent. He thinks it'll run true to form and won't expect any change in character and that's his downfall. Snap! The fly is caught."

"Granddad watches quite a bit of television for company," Sally said, passing him a piece of Flora's homemade spice cake.

"You can't beat real company Blackie. Would you mind if I call in to see you when I come up to do my training at the Old Mill? I'll enjoy getting beaten by you at chess," Cuthbert asked. "I'm sure Sally would be happier," he said, and Sally nodded, brushing cake crumbs off her yellow jumper.

Sally had luxuriant brown hair, gentle eyes and a smile that brought her into focus. Her breasts were large and shapely but they carried a sign, *Do not disturb*.

"You'll be very welcome. One thing in life I have always followed, Cuthbert, is to always be careful but not cautious. Caution breeds fear and fear breeds an inability to act. Lack of action could destroy you."

Chapter Fourteen

AFTER BEDE PARKED THE VAN UP AGAINST THE FACTORY GATE HE dragged the bag of tools from the back and they both slipped on balaclavas and gloves.

Dolly took the electronic key from the bag and slipped the alligator clips on to the terminals as Bede watched. The yellow light turned the circle of numbered bulbs and stopped. "One," Bede mouthed, "Zero, Six, Six." Suddenly the green light came on.

"Bingo," Dolly said as she unclipped the device and opened the gate. After she repeated the process on the unit door she started to smile.

"Something tickling you Dolly?"

"What idiot, after spending thousands of pounds on electric locks, has both codes the same: ten sixty six? Two heavy duty Chub locks would have been more secure."

Once inside the huge heavy-plastic interlocking inner doors, Dolly put her finger to her lips to motion for Bede to keep quiet. They both stood in silence in the near darkness. Bede moved closer to her, drawn in by a faint aroma of her perfume. In the moonlight he could clearly make out her facial features, her short cropped natural blonde hair and the dusting of freckles highlighted by her faint tan.

She pulled a long silver box from the bag, set a distance and frequency on the viewfinder screen, plugged in the headphones and turned a three hundred and sixty degrees sweep. Dolly stood up and pulled off the goggles and headphones. "Clean, totally clean," she said, then walked over to a wall light panel and flood lit the building.

"There are no audio security units but still watch out for wired pressure pads Bede, I can't see them but square black pads could set off a pressure monitored alarm."

Dolly pulled a set of plans from the bag and spread them over a conveyor belt.

"The upstairs is made up of toilets, changing rooms and offices, so if they are making or storing anything illegal it will be down here." A lone pigeon flapped its wings trying to find an escape route and unsettled them. Dolly handed Bede a slim slide camera.

"Just push the whole mechanism in and out, each movement will take a photograph. You circle around left and I will circle right," she instructed. Within minutes Dolly had come upon a production line bench holding explosives, land mines, stun grenades and time bombs. Everything was photographed and logged. The place was a cottage industry which marketed widows and orphans.

Dolly and Bede met up at a pair of large see through plastic doors, clearly marked as unsafe and taped off. This was like red rag to a bull, and Dolly started removing the yellow and black tape, "I wonder what is really behind these doors," she mused.

"Be careful Dolly," Bede warned, "Remember what Cuthbert said about it being an old building."

Dolly pushed open the doors and went head long through the floor and down, deep down and out of sight inside an old well.

Bede shouted in vain, she gave no reply and things looked bad. He ran upstairs to the stores, found a long coiled rope and brought it down, tying one end around his waist and the other to a cut off electrical post. In Dolly's hessian bag he found a small but powerful head lamp and switched it on. He started climbing down through the rotten floor boards; every two minutes he stopped, took a breath, and called out to Dolly, hoping for a moan or the sound of her breathing.

He stopped when he heard a faint moan. Using his feet to guide him he moved over towards the wall. He couldn't see Dolly but he could smell her, a faint smell of hope, and then he felt Dolly's shoe.

She was upside down and her jacket was caught on something. He had no idea how injured she was or how on earth he could right her and raise her up, but he knew time and speed was of the utmost importance. He could hear the snagged clothing start to tear.

He slipped a pair of handcuffs onto Dolly's wrists and put her arms over his head. He then slowly pulled her up to an upright position and with an unbelievable amount of strength pulled her up out of the hole and on to a patch of solid flooring. He rolled her on to her back and started breathing air into her mouth and then pounded on her back.

Suddenly a rush of air and dust was forced out of Dolly's mouth as she regained consciousness.

"Don't move," Bede shouted, pulling himself up, "you may have broken something."

Dolly slowly pulled herself onto her knees and then started to breathe again. Looking at Bede with the rope and head lamp still turned on she started to laugh hysterically.

Bede stood looking at her not knowing whether to laugh or cry.

"You," Dolly stopped and took another breath, "climbed down, pulled me up and risked your own life." Dolly struggled to put two words together as she was in a state of shock

"I just tried…" Bede started and Dolly, seeing he was becoming emotional, reached out with both arms and hugged him.

"Thank you George," she whispered, "you saved my life."

Back in the car, Dolly put her hands to her head, "The cameras George, what about the cameras?"

Bede pulled both cameras from his pocket, "Don't panic Dolly, everything's sorted and the photographs are logged."

Chapter Fifteen

AFTER AN EARLY BREAKFAST AND A RUN ALONG THE HARBOUR, Cuthbert entered the hotel HQ to make an early start and look over the previous day's door to door interviews.

Dolly was already in and scanning earlier CCTV footage. Her face was badly bruised. "How did last night go, any connections with the van or the murder? Have you cut your head Dolly?"

"Send Bede in to see me when he turns up," Dolly snapped "and I still haven't got any feedback from that McDuff." She picked up her coffee and went into her own small personal office. Cuthbert knew Dolly's mood could change with the weather, he sensed her barometer was on 'thunder and stormy'. He took his coffee and stood in the hotel's doorway, spying Bede sat in his car, motionless.

Cuthbert tapped on Bede's window and could see his thumbs turning one against the other.

"You joining us today Sergeant?" He asked.

"Just thinking about the case sir," Bede answered, getting out of the car and locking the door.

"Dolly wants to see you," Cuthbert said, "I'm off to catch McDuff then I'm taking Seamus up to Glasgow to identify Paddy.

Then I'm meeting Big Sam, so I will be gone most of the morning."

Bede nodded and Cuthbert crossed the road to McDuff's cottage. He pushed open the weathered wrought iron gate with the name *The Rook* standing out proudly. He ignored the front door and skirted round to the back, where McDuff was busy cleaning out one of his canary cages.

"Can I have a moment of your time please? It's nothing to worry about," Cuthbert asked, wanting to make it clear that this visit had nothing to do with his earlier washing line exploits. "It's this murder of the Irish lad on Friday at the hotel. Seeing as you live across the road I thought you may have witnessed something."

"About half nine," McDuff started, "this young girl, the barmaid, she came out. I never noticed the lad but he was slumped on the bench drunk or whatever and she walked up behind him and pushed a broken glass into his neck. She never said a Dickey Bird, just stuck it into his neck and showed her teeth when she did it. Then she went back in through the French doors and came back out a couple of minutes later. She just put her bag over her shoulder and walked off as cool as a cucumber."

"She didn't break the glass outside?" Cuthbert asked.

"No, it was already broken," McDuff answered and continued to tend to his birds.

"You never thought to come forward with this information to one of my officers?"

"Well no one asked me," McDuff smiled.

"Before that," Cuthbert asked, "say half an hour earlier?"

"No I would have been out here, I put them to bed then so no, I didn't see anything then." McDuff answered.

"You'll need to make a statement and if you do think of anything else please let us know," Cuthbert left to pick up Seamus.

Cuthbert knew Glasgow well as he had spent his early years with Strathclyde police. Firstly he was escorted by senior officers and then later he teamed up with fellow cadet Pete Marino.

Cuthbert knew Glasgow's secrets and its breeding grounds for the next batch of criminals. He knew Glasgow could never answer you, would not know you. Glasgow could turn its back on you and lock you out, leaving you in a vagrant mood with its depth of poverty and depression, but he also knew Glasgow had a wealth of pride, dignity and a zest for life.

So it was to Glasgow Cuthbert brought Seamus, parking the Bentley behind the granite carved building of Glasgow's High Court. In the corner of the car park, hidden away out of sight, sat the small single storey weathered stone building with the inviting word *Mortuary* above the main doorway.

Many had come before with grief to collect and take away the offal of death, no niceties, just taking away the mask of death.

Inside Cuthbert led Seamus across the shiny polished floor to a second set of double glass doors. At one side hung a brass bell with a sign, *ring once*. An attendant came to the door and pressed a buzzer to allow Cuthbert to enter.

"You just sit a minute Seamus and I will come for you," Cuthbert said. Seamus seemed in a different world, like a puppet being led by its puppeteer.

Cuthbert liked Eddy the mortuary attendant, he always found him polite and professional and talked about his big passion, his country and western nights out. He wore all the outfits, the spurs, hat and pistol and went to special ho-downs. But there would be no ho-down today for Seamus.

As Eddie washed down a white metal table, water sluiced down runnels at the edges and onto the floor. They shaped a ritual as always with no words being spoken, no conversation, just a quick look into the face of death and a nod of the head.

Cuthbert knew death, especially sudden death. A sudden death gave totally different reactions from relatives or loved ones. For some it deformed their dreams and others it stunned them beyond belief. While some would weep for days or even weeks, others talked nonstop, apportioning blame, justifying, explaining some hysterical notion. Some stayed silent and dignified, others outraged as grief gave them a hunger for retribution.

Seamus stood at one side of Paddy's head and Eddie at the other, Paddy had been wrapped in a cheese cloth material like a mummy with a flap at his face for identification. It was all official and it was all dignified. In disbelief Seamus simply nodded and then shook his head before being led back through the double doors. It had been like the dead mirrored by the dead. With no emotion Seamus began to repeat some Gaelic and then silence. In the Bentley Cuthbert unscrewed a bottle of Arran Special and passed it to him. After finishing the half bottle Seamus's head rolled to one side and he was away, sound asleep. It had been too much to take, first his father murdered barely twelve months ago when supposedly trying to escape and now Paddy.

Cuthbert parked up at the corner of St Andrew's Street and Turnbull Street with Seamus dreaming of a different world on the Bentley's back seat. He entered the Chief Inspector of Constabulary's office.

"You wanted to see me sir?"

"Yes Durham, I had forgotten what you looked like," The Chief, Gordon Cowley, rose from his seat and started to pace the floor. *Yes,* Cuthbert thought, *Like Rommel, the Desert Fox addressing the Africa Corps before engaging The Eighth Army.*

"Sometimes Durham I feel like I'm caught in the cross hairs of a sniper's telescopic sight. It's strange," the Chief went on, "when other officers come before me I always have a feeling of enlightenment and confidence, but after seeing you I get a deep down feeling of despair and non-co operation."

"Remember one thing sir," Durham answered, "all of your officers based here have a charming presence and I always have a charming absence," and with that he left.

When Cuthbert returned to the Bentley Seamus was standing, slightly hunched, leaning against the car door. On seeing Cuthbert, Seamus rushed towards him and hugged him.

"Cuthbert I woke up I didn't know where I was," Cuthbert patted his back, unsure what to do. He had seen bereavement too often, different people cope with death, especially a violent death, in different ways.

"Why Paddy?" Seamus asked.

"I can't answer that Seamus, no one can, we just have to remember Paddy, think of his good times and get on with life."

Chapter Sixteen

THE CHIEF INSPECTOR ENTERED THE STATION'S MAIN DOORS. Naylor was still on duty and still conferring with Mary Franks.

"Do you ever go home Naylor? Any progress on the kestrels?"

"Yes sir. The question didn't stipulate if the kestrels were alive or dead, so one could be dead on the roof but still counting. Basically there could be no kestrels on the roof, if the dead one had fallen off and the other had flown away, or only one kestrel, or two kestrels with one still sitting on the roof and the other being dead but still on the roof."

"Well done Naylor."

"Big Sam Harris contacted me sir," Mary Franks piped up, "and asked me if I would be interested in being part of the judging team for Biggar show. Old Sandy died."

"Well Mary, I would give it some thought, because even though everyone has confidence in you, you must ask yourself if you want to do it and if you have the time. It is a big responsibility, villagers have spent twelve months preparing something for the show and your swift judgment will make them a winner or not."

Cuthbert had arranged to see Sam in his office and was surprised not to see his light burning.

Seeing the main examining room's light on Cuthbert went to the locker area and changed into his scrubs, overalls, overshoes, gloves and mask. He was knocked for six when he entered the room and Sam turned out to be a woman. The body she was working on was more bone than body.

"You are DCI Durham I take it? I am Gertrude Jeckel. Sam asked me to pass on a message, apparently Lurch has found some particulates in the victim's hair."

"Particulates?" Cuthbert repeated.

"Feathers, small down feathers," she said.

Could they be canary feathers? He pondered, now thinking about McDuff living only yards from where the victim was killed.

"So you are one of those who boil the bones to find out a dead body's past?" Cuthbert asked.

"You surprise me Chief Inspector, I thought you would have known better. The old methods of using flora and fauna combined with modern technology to ascertain the identity of a person is virtually fool proof."

"I must apologise, but I am more used to the recent body examinations, work done by the pathologist."

"Let me show you something," she said, handing him a set of twelve photographs."

"This is where my specimen was found, close to Kemin Bay."

"So this is the gentleman who wandered off from the retirement home last month," Cuthbert surmised.

"How on earth do you know?"

"Yes it was a stupid thing to say," he concluded.

"First thing I do when I arrive at the site of the body is to look for signs from the surrounding plants, soil and insects," she pointed to the first photograph. "If the soil under the body has a high iron content it would suggest the body had bled out. If the body showed signs of a trauma or a cut and the soil content was low in iron this would suggest the victim had been cut after death or murdered elsewhere and then left there.

"Flies are attracted to the body by smell. Within the hour they lay eggs which turn to pupae, now the colour of these is very important to determine the time of death. The darker the pupae the older it is." She pointed to the second photograph.

"The larvae on this body are mainly blowflies, bluebottles and green bottles. As you can see from the third photograph there are no pupae husks around the body so no pupae had hatched. As the life cycle of the flies is fourteen days it suggests the time of death is under that time period, probably between ten and twelve days."

"Very impressive," Cuthbert said.

"Now after the body has been removed, see in this photograph, this yellow-white substance that has killed the grass? It is a by-product of decomposition called adipocere or grave wax. It is a soap formed from the body's fatty acids as the muscle proteins break down, this makes the soil highly alkaline, which in turn kills the grass.

"If the adipocere is brittle and crumbly it suggests a rapid decomposition and if the adipocere is softer it suggests a slower decomposition, possibly from cooler dryer weather. Now, getting a time of death is important but it does not identify the deceased. If you look at the last photograph…" she pointed.

"The dry leaves?" Cuthbert asked.

"When a body has been dead for some time you start getting skin slippage, giving it that wrinkled appearance, particularly the hands. The skin has sloughed off completely, like a glove." She handed him a see-through plastic evidence bag containing the dry crisp tissue.

"Prints could not be taken from this?" He said incredulously.

"Soaked overnight it will rehydrate then slip on to a hand like a glove."

"So much can be discovered from a body and the surrounding area, but where do forensic anthropologists learn these things?"

"I studied at a research facility in Tennessee called the Body Farm," she informed him.

Lurch was looking through the comparison microscope when Cuthbert came in.

"*Pavo Cristatus,*" Lurch announced, "Peacock Indian Blue. I found, well let me rephrase that, I was meant to find, the tiny feathers on his clothing and hair and small traces of cotton, probably from a pillow or cushion."

"Planted," Cuthbert asked and Lurch nodded.

"Something else, a military tie," Lurch wound it around his hand. "Not something you can just buy from a shop. It is a DLI tie, the Durham's, with a serial number of the owner."

"So we can find the owner?"

"Something else too, the broken glass had traces of bitumen, or road tar," Lurch said.

Sam passed Cuthbert the official report. Paddy was cut with a champagne glass deeper than what the preliminary report showed. The scraping revealed fine shards of crystal glass. Sam read from the report: *Laceration is macerated but not significant, contusion with a small laceration below the ear.*

"The lack of blood shows he was already dead. Jinty didn't kill him," Sam concluded. "The skin around his lower neck was bruised suggesting a huge amount of pressure had been used."

"By a tall, very strong male?" Cuthbert interrupted.

"It is amazing what secrets a body can tell us long after death. After the brain was weighed and inspected and the skull was boiled I found something remarkable. This murderer is very cunning. He stuck a glass in the neck to hide the fact they had already broken his neck, a bluff. But that is not the end of the story."

"Double bluff," Cuthbert again interrupted.

"The heavy bruising on the skin was just that, there were no breaks whatsoever. The back of the skull had been hit with tremendous force in one particular area, sending a small piece of bone into the brain. Death was instantaneous." Sam again read from the autopsy report: *Haematoma in the subdural space consistent with a subdural bleed. Hernitation of the uncinate process on the same side.* He went on, "Death was caused by a palpable fracture of the neck caused by a tremendous blow to the back of the head causing curable contusions beneath the skull fracture. The killer knew what he was doing; he knew the amount of force needed and also the direction of force."

"So this now changes the build of the killer?" Cuthbert asked and Sam nodded.

Chapter Seventeen

CUTHBERT STOPPED OUTSIDE THE SCHOOL WHEN HE SAW SALLY Harris waiting for the bus.

"That girl," he pointed to a young girl, "her with the pig tail, does she go to this school? Do you know her?"

"Yes, that's Poppy, Poppy Mcillvinney, she's been doing a poetry class with the after school club."

Cuthbert recognised her as the girl he had seen in a recurring dream being murdered beside the Celtic stone on the moor. "Fancy a hot bowl of soup at the Portpatrick Harbour Bar? Maybe a hot toddy in front of the roaring log fire?" Cuthbert asked through the Bentley window. Without answering Sally pounced on the huge leather upholstery and within a moment was sitting as he had said, in front of a log fire with a hot toddy, a large bowl of best Scottish broth and a huge piece of crusty buttered bread.

"How's Raymond, at school I mean?" Cuthbert asked.

"Not good," she answered. "He doesn't get on with one of the teachers, Peter Lumsden, the sports teacher. He's been using Raymond as a punch bag and his ribs are black and blue. I've seen his headmistress Miss Hunter but she says without proof it's Raymond's word against his."

"Well I think I might have a word with Mr Lumsden, I've been looking for a sparring partner for the Biggar show."

"I thought it might do Raymond good to go down to the labs and see what goes on. If he knows he'll need good grades at school it might spur him to stick in at it. Anything else he likes?" Cuthbert asked, topping up Sally's glass with mulled wine, "Any hobbies or interests?"

"Photography, old cameras believe it or not. Where he gets that from I don't know. Where would I find an old camera?" Sally shrugged.

Cuthbert smiled.

Chapter Eighteen

DOLLY WAS HARD AT WORK WHEN SERGEANT GEORGE BEDE ENtered her office.

"You wanted to see me?"

"Yes George, first of all I want to thank you for saving my life. I'm going to recommend you for a Police bravery award so you get recognition for your actions. I'm proud of you."

Bede reddened and turned away, it was rare for a boy from the Drum to receive this kind of praise.

"Sit down George, I want to show you something." As Bede sat opposite she produced an electronic device from her bag.

"But I thought you threw that into the Irish Sea?" Bede queried.

"What I threw into the sea was a live grenade, this is simply a mish mash of cardboard and wires a child could see through," she said. "I knew the commander was away on holiday so for a bit of fun I set out to make you look a dummy, a joke. Then you go and save my life. Who's the fool now?" Dolly said with a tear in her eye. "If you want to file a complaint I don't blame you, you deserve better. You've proved that."

Bede sat, near speechless, "I don't want to put in a complaint

Dolly, you are the last person in the world I would think of as a fool. In fact what you did, coming over on top of me that day at the terminal was… well, it's the closest I will ever feel to spiritualism, being close to death and also being close to life. No, let's keep this to ourselves and learn from it. We still have to work together and move on," Bede said, and they shook hands.

"I will never forget what you did George, thank you," Dolly kissed him.

Cuthbert and Bede turned up on Portpatrick beach with the wind starting to pick up, blowing the dry sand into their faces. It had been a dog walker who had found the body at first light. As they approached they could see Constables Franks and Jolly standing over the body. Standing over them in turn was Commander Hamilton pointing a revolver.

"Franks radioed in earlier sir, from the minivan," Bede said. "Responded to a dog walker's phone call about finding a man's body on the beach. Apparently a blue sealed drum had also been washed onto the beach with funny writing. She says it looks Chinese."

"That makes life a lot easier," Cuthbert said, "we will have to close off the whole beach for health and safety reasons."

"Hamilton, put down that weapon!" The Chief Inspector yelled above the now strengthening wind, "before someone gets hurt. You will look silly with the Colt Taurus stuck somewhere the sun don't shine."

"This man works for me," Hamilton explained. "The home office now takes precedent on this beach."

Once Hamilton had lowered his pistol Cuthbert grabbed him by the neck and frogmarched him into the sea, dousing his head underneath the raging white froth.

"The beach is now a restricted area for everyone Hamilton, a suspicious possibly toxic container has contaminated the area."

Bede rushed forward, pulled Hamilton's head from beneath the water and dragged him onto the dry sand. He was struggling to breath, gasping for air.

"You're a mad man Durham, you could have killed me!" An exasperated Hamilton said, coughing sea water onto the sand.

"Close off the beach George." Cuthbert ordered. "Put Jolly at one end and Franks at the other. I will sort out Big Sam and the Scene of Crime Unit. I will seek information on the barrel from the Scientific Advisor and Hazardous Materials Officer."

"Sounds like lethal stuff sir," Bede commented.

"The letters on the drum are Mandarin," Cuthbert said, smiling. "It's cooking oil, but Hamilton doesn't know that."

Cuthbert drove to the Portpatrick Hotel and saw Sean painting a new car park sign.

"Very nice Sean," he commented. "How are the swimming lessons going with Dolly?"

"I think she was thrown out of the Gestapo for cruelty Cuthbert, she's very demanding and keeps telling me that one day it might save my life." Cuthbert smiled as he entered the main doors.

"Hello, I am Chief Inspector Cuthbert Durham and you must be Mrs Diep Nhan," Cuthbert asked the mature Vietnamese receptionist.

"It's actually Miss Nhan Diep," she replied, "but please call me Diep."

Cuthbert knew that having money wasn't the same as having class, and the woman he had just met seemed well in possession of both. She was very slender and willowy with grey hair in an elfin cut that suited her delicate features. She wore expensive jeans and a light maroon sweater and very little jewellery, just pearl ear studs and a very delicate ornate brooch in the shape of a dragon.

"You are a beautiful woman Diep," Cuthbert commented. "I wonder if I could ask your advice on a police matter?"

"You are a respected man Chief Inspector," Diep noted. "I have heard many stories from the villagers. Some years ago I worked as a criminal profiler trained in psychological profiling for the Saigon Police Division. I know basic police procedure. How can I help you?" she asked.

Cuthbert was impressed with her credentials and pulled his note book from his pocket.

"A blue drum was washed up this morning on to the beach and it had these words painted on its side," He showed her the letters.

"It was exported from Beijing Engineering and it is fine oil, hydraulic oil I think you call it," Diep explained.

A large grin came over Cuthbert's face.

"Did I say something funny Mr Policeman?"

"No not at all," Cuthbert explained, "I told my Sergeant it was frying oil, cooking oil. Maybe we could meet sometime for a meal and you could explain the benefits of psychological profiling in solving a case. Do you live in the village?"

"No, in Durham, in the shadow of the great Cathedral on the riverbank in Prebands Cottage. You would love my *Com Tay Cam* Chicken made in a clay pot with *Nuoc Mom* Sauce."

"Sounds divine Diep, and thank you for the translation. There was one other thing: as you know, we are investigating the death of a young man in the Japanese garden. The tapes from the CCTV cameras have been examined and we found the camera covering the back stairs from the top floor down to the kitchen went blank for just over thirty three minutes at the time of the murder. With you being on duty monitoring the screens that night I wondered, did you notice a problem?"

"The cameras were all working on the night but someone may have simply put a lens cap over the camera and then taken it off," she explained.

"But why would someone do that?" Cuthbert asked.

"Perhaps the man who murdered the Irishman was inside the hotel in one of the upstairs rooms," Diep suggested.

"Did you have any spare rooms on the night of the murder?"

"Everything was fully booked up except for the Bridal Suite," she said.

"Do you have the key for it so we can take a look?"

"We don't lock that room as we sometimes store things in there," she answered.

As Cuthbert followed her up the stairs he wondered why *he* hadn't thought of someone being in the hotel waiting for the opportunity to kill Paddy.

"Someone has definitely been in here, the bed would not have been made that way and the soap has been used," Diep said.

"Yes Diep, I think you are right. Someone may well have been in here the night Paddy was killed."

Diep was trying to pull something from behind the bed.

"*Thien nga,*" she said, pointing, "*Thien nga.*"

"Pillow," Cuthbert translated, "Cushion."

"Thien nga," Diep was getting frustrated, unable to move it. Cuthbert edged the huge bed forward and pulled the pillow out.

"A swan," He said, pushing it into an evidence bag. He turned the stuffed bird until its head was facing him and read the embroidered message beneath the bird's neck: *Victor in Europe 1945.*

"I do not understand what the words mean," Diep said, confused.

"It would have read *Victory* when it was made in nineteen forty five, but some little boy must have picked out the thread from the Y letter," Cuthbert explained, inspecting the swan very closely. "I think there are small specks of blood on the head. If we identify the blood we may trace the killer," he said.

"I think you may need a psychological profile of this girl you are holding," she said.

"You worked with this girl, have you spoken to her?" Cuthbert asked.

"I worked downtown for Saigon police, Saigon is a cross roads for many travellers of different nations speaking many languages. I was capable of forming a profile on potential drug dealers and people traffickers not by speaking but by…" She stopped, frustrated by being unable to find the English translation. "*Ban nang can dam,*" she made a fist and hit her stomach.

"Gut instinct," Cuthbert motioned, pointing to his stomach.

Diep smiled, releasing the worry lines from her face. Cuthbert reached over and put his hand on her arm. "You look so beautiful when you smile."

Diep pulled her arm away quickly and stood up. "I must be getting back to the desk," she made her way downstairs to the sanctuary of her small reception area.

"I am sorry," Cuthbert apologised.

"What I was saying is important, she will make a show of being vulnerable and weak but she is planning her next move," she explained. "You ask her when she last ate. She will say 'I know exactly, I didn't have a watch but it was still light but about to get dark or it might have been dark about to get light'. Now you are more confused than you were at the start."

As Cuthbert left the hotel's main door he noticed Sally in the car park, she had brought Sean a tall glass of orange juice with ice bobbing up and down in it. He waved to her, thinking that exactly one week ago it was a champagne glass carried by a woman that had caused so much distress.

He cut across the golf course to get to the beach, the wind was even stronger and was blowing the tape Pandora and Polly Anna were unrolling. Big Sam was positioning the scientific support van high up the beach onto some firmer sand, away from the incoming tide.

Cuthbert waved and like magic they all waved back together. Bede came over to meet him.

"No Hamilton?" Cuthbert asked.

"Made a right scene sir," Bede replied "and insisted on an ambulance but there has been no sign of the hazardous materials people."

"No the council's sorting it," Cuthbert replied, "it was as I thought, just oil."

"Do you want me to help you with that George?"

"With what sir?" Bede answered.

"With that weight you are carrying across your shoulders."

"Is it that obvious sir?"

"Everything at home all right George? You've not been yourself the last few days and you've been asking for night shift."

"We seem to be pulling in different directions sir, Lisa and I," Bede answered, "Even Jonathon doesn't say much now."

"Try and find what makes them tick George," Cuthbert advised, "Any hobbies?"

"Lisa used to sing," Bede informed him. "When I first met her she was singing for charity and Jonathon keeps asking me to get him a camera, an old one."

"Well," Cuthbert smiled, "the Biggar show is coming up so get Lisa to practice a song and I'll loan you a camera and Jonathon can enter a photograph."

Bede smiled, he knew his boss worried about him and it made him feel wanted.

Chapter Nineteen

CUTHBERT PARKED THE BENTLEY OUTSIDE THE SCHOOL IN Stranraer and entered the gym, where Miss Hunter was patiently waiting for him. She was in her early sixties, short and dumpy and dressed in a pair of patterned brocade curtains topped off with a white bow in her hair. She looked as innocent as a letter home to mother.

"I know this looks like a gym, Chief Inspector, but it is also used for assembly meetings and Christmas parties. This big trunk houses our life experience case," she explained. "If a student has done some exceptional work writing a story or a poem we put it in here."

"Did Jinty Ferguson have work in there?" Cuthbert asked, "Was she talented?"

"Yes she was very talented," she reached inside and brought out a poem. "She told me she used to go with her mum and dad to the dry rocks, a nice riverside picnic area near Glenluce. She wrote this poem about it."

"Very neat hand writing," Cuthbert commented. "This photograph of the school children, is she on this?" he asked.

"Yes, the second row in the middle," Miss Hunter said.

"This girl behind her with the birthmark beneath her eye…"

"That is Domenica Hannah, she was expelled for assaulting a fellow pupil after this photograph was taken. She said the girl had been staring at her."

"Did this Domenica have a poem in the life experience case?"

"Well yes, I objected to it going in but the English teacher said it was art."

"Can I take a copy of this poem?" She nodded and reluctantly handed him a copy.

"Why did no one believe Jinty when she complained about being bullied by Domenica?" "It was a long time ago and we didn't know if the injuries were self inflicted."

"What, she kicked herself in the face? Now that would be difficult. Would it be possible to see the school's medical officer, Mr Spikings?"

"Jack is on sick leave; in fact he may have to consider early retirement."

"Because of his failing eyesight?" Asked Cuthbert, "Is that why he could not see the bruises on Raymond Harris's back? His doctor told me he was lucky he wasn't crippled for life."

"You have to realise that children have active minds, that boys fall out of trees and blame a teacher for their injuries. That girls fall in love with a teacher and to get his attention report that he has touched her."

"So did Jinty and her parents go to Australia to get away from her bully, Miss Hunter?"

"Off the record yes," she started to cry. "Her father came to me and said he hoped Jinty's new teachers in Australia would look after her properly."

"Would she have written this herself?"

"Oh yes, definitely, and signed."

Cuthbert opened the freshly painted door to the Gym; it bore the name *P. Lumsden, Teacher*. He sat in the boys' changing rooms at the back of the gym, unfolded the poem and read the lines out loud.

Painted Black
By Domenica Hannah

No baby Jesus doves of peace
Holy fishes on the back
Forget the peace and love they sell
I want it painted black

No holy bible at midnight mass
Let's just keep them for the quack
'Cause I live here in the real world
I want it painted black

No early morning sunshine
It's the devil's midnight pack
Darkness is the mask I wear
I want it painted black

Sisters of mercy I have met
Tied me down on my back
Benediction, Catechism and Absolutions
For God's sake paint it black

Cuthbert's nostrils picked up a scent that only boys' changing rooms can give; a slight smell of gloss paint was also detected.

"Can I help you sir?" An overweight bald headed man stood in the doorway.

"I hope so, I'm Chief Inspector Cuthbert Durham from Strathclyde Constabulary," he took his warrant card from his inside pocket. "The fact is I'm quite a keen boxer and do a bit training and sparring at the Old Mill Club. I got a message that a certain Mr Lumsden here at the school might give me a few tips on punch bag work as he's good with his fists."

"Boxing? No, sorry to disappoint you Chief Inspector, I'm more for table tennis and tiddly winks," Mr Lumsden answered.

"So there is no truth in what I've been hearing that you treated young Raymond Harris like a punch bag?" His smile seemed to lose its sparkle. "One thing I pride myself on is that I never get angry, but I've failed this time. I hate bullies who use young children as punch bags. You ever hear of health and safety Mr Lumsden? Have a look at that soap on the shower base."

The teacher turned and shook his head, and on turning back, *bang!* Cuthbert hit his chin with an uppercut, then *bang! bang! bang!* three more jabs to the ribs. He crumpled into the base of the shower, groaning. Cuthbert picked up a bar of soap from a holder and threw it into the shower.

"What did I say arsehole? Don't slip on the soap," Cuthbert turned on the hot water tap and left the changing rooms to the sound of screaming.

The church bell was just chiming seven when Cuthbert dropped Sally at her grandfather's. "Don't worry about Raymond, with Seamus teaching him boxing and Dolly the taekwondo he's in good hands. We'll be back for nine," Cuthbert promised.

Seamus and Dolly were sat on the thick protective training mat when Cuthbert and young Raymond came in. A couple of young boys were working out on the big bag, another on the small punch ball and two were skipping, all being watched by Seb, Sebastian Macready.

"This is Raymond, Raymond Harris," Cuthbert said, "and this big lump is Seamus, Seamus O' Connell, but better known in the world of boxing as the Mad Irishman. This is Dorothy Malone, she's really a princess but tonight's her night off," they reached out to shake Raymond's hand.

"I'm not a child, I'm ten years old and should be treated as such!"

"You best get away Cuthbert, I can see he's not even warmed up yet," Seamus said.

Cuthbert waved and left to the sound of Dolly starting the warming up exercises.

Back at the station Cuthbert found Naylor alone sat at the desk reading a comic.

"Is Mary not in tonight Sergeant?" Cuthbert asked.

"She's in the rest room sir, looking through old police books."

"Here's a question for you Nat, one to think on, I don't need an answer tonight. In the horror film, which character was seven feet tall and had a bolt through his neck?" He asked.

"Frankenstein," Naylor interrupted.

"Naylor, what did I say? Wait until the morning and confer with Mary."

Chapter Twenty

ANDERS ANDERSON STOOD AT THE END OF CUTHBERT'S DRIVE watching the new structure being lowered into position.

"What's this then Anders, are you downsizing or is this a warhead for your rocket?" Cuthbert asked.

"It's called a Pod and cost over ten thousand pounds. It can tell you the time and temperature in any country. I have been lax with security and have been getting visitors in the night, but when I get International Security housed in the new pod I will sleep sounder at night."

"They sound professional," Cuthbert noted.

"Ex-spies that can pull down and kill a water buffalo bare-handed," Anders smiled.

"I don't think we get many water buffalo on the moor."

"I have an old couple coming up from London, the Dickinsons, they are thinking of buying the chalet. They are into all this Druid crap."

"You seen these posters on the lamp posts about the old chap lost on the moor?" Cuthbert asked.

"Yes, I heard he was a town crier in Glasgow in his youth."

Suddenly an old Morris van drove towards them out of control, Anders dived for cover.

"Sorry cobber but the steering is shot. Do you mind if I bring a couple of Sheilas back for the party tonight? The name's Bruce."

"Listen Bruce you're here to look after the site," Anders told him, "Meaning no drinks, food, drugs or girls. And keep an eye out for a town crier on the moor."

Cuthbert held the white sheet he had taken from the airing cupboard and waited for Bruce to settle in. He watched him go to the back of the van and open the rear door. Two young girls climbed out of the back wearing roller skates, shorts and matching t-shirts with the slogan "Black Bush Whiskey." Bruce followed them back carrying a small barrel of Bonsai Beer.

Cuthbert crept behind the pod and up the steep wooden staircase, pulled the sheet over his head and started to moan very loudly.

It was Bruce who came out first, dressed in a bright yellow vest, and then the two girls wearing only their pants. The girls shone their torches up the staircase and focused the beams on the sheet, Cuthbert raised his arms high and bellowed, "Twelve o' clock and all is well in Bearsden tonight!"

Bruce and the two girls ran to the van. Cuthbert watched it weave from side to side up the road. He walked down the staircase and into the pod to find three steaks cooking on a potable barbecue. He turned the three gas burners to full power and turned on the Pod's computer.

Suddenly a girl's voice came from the speakers: "The temperature in the Pod is twenty nine degrees the time is twelve thirty three."

Cuthbert sat in the garden playing his guitar and watching his two catfish enjoying the music. He could just make out the sound of the flames licking the side of the pod. The girl's voice was booming over the moor: "The temperature in the pod is four thousand degrees and the weather in downtown Miami is hot and stormy."

Suddenly the pod exploded as the gas bottles from the barbecue blew.

Chapter Twenty-One

"POLICE PROCEDURES DURING INTERVIEWS?" CUTHBERT ASKED.

"Yes sir, if you think I'm up to it," Constable Carolyn Jolly replied.

"Yes I do," he reassured her. "We'll get started on the Arab. But one thing I want to make clear Carolyn, the questioning is in connection with Patrick Dolan only. At no time do you mention the factory or anything away from the Portpatrick area. We mustn't frighten him off, he is the bait for a bigger fish."

Cuthbert sat next to Jolly as Naylor brought Imran in.

"I've made some tea," Nathan said, looking at the Arab "I thought you might like a cup."

Imran drank the first cup, started on a second and ate the full plate of biscuits.

"I only have one question for you," Cuthbert started, "and my colleague, Constable Jolly, may also have one. On the Thursday last week your friend Jamil and yourself were in the bar of the Portpatrick Hotel. While there your friend had an argument with an Irishman called Patrick Dolan. Were you or your friend in or near the same hotel the following night, the Friday?"

"No, I can honestly say, no, we sailed together to Moscow and we had an important meeting on the Saturday night with two brothers, I mean two customers, it was very important that we made the meeting," Imran said.

"Thank you for your time and your honesty," Cuthbert responded, "any question you wish to put to Imran, Constable?"

"Yes, did you get the contract, Imran?" The Constable asked.

"Yes, we got the contract, we were happy," Imran looked up and was escorted to the front doors by Jolly. When she was back Cuthbert poured her a cup of tea.

"Well, I'm afraid there are no biscuits left. What did you think of him?" He asked.

"I think he'd been warned what not to say. He realised he'd crossed that line when he said they'd seen brothers, not customers."

"Yes, I thought that he stumbled there too. Well, it's been a long day Jolly, what time do you finish?"

"I have to work one more hour sir."

"You live nearby, don't you Carolyn?" Cuthbert asked.

"Yes sir, near the Ferry Terminal," she answered.

"Come on, drink your tea, I'll drop you off. I'll pass your cottage on my way up to the Old Mill Road. You've earned your parole," he paused, thoughtful for a moment, "I have been thinking about putting you forward for promotion Carolyn, do you think you could take on the extra responsibility?" Cuthbert asked.

"Oh yes sir, yes indeed."

Everyone was leaving and getting into a mini bus when Cuthbert walked into the Old Mill Club. Raymond and Dolly were still busy doing a 'cat dan she dan' with Dolly shouting instructions. Seamus came over to see him.

"How has Raymond been tonight?" Cuthbert asked.

"He's a bit stiff and took some time to warm him up but he's keen to learn," Seamus answered.

"You alright now Seamus?" Cuthbert asked.

"Just ticking over."

"There is a question I must ask you, Seamus, I don't want to but… was Paddy running guns?"

"I thought you would ask, no, it was definitely animal feed."

"If we could just find his van…" Cuthbert concluded, then changed the subject, "What do you think of Dolly?"

"She's some girl Cuthbert, I like her. She wears a crash helmet on the outside but inside she's a pussy cat."

"I have a surprise for her tonight, she is meeting a man who has the same IQ as her and is a top chess master. I think she needs a mental challenge."

"I promised her a run on the Triumph and a rip around the bay on board the King Billy. Sean is making kebabs for when we get back."

"Sounds like you've both found a friend Seamus, the chess can wait. Enjoy tonight, after what you and Sean have had to put up with recently you deserve it," Cuthbert pulled a bottle of Arran Special from his pocket and handed it to Seamus.

Next morning the wind was bracing, blowing in off the sea. He'd forgotten how strong and cold the wind could be in this part of south west Scotland. The fishermen had said a storm was brewing.

Sally and Raymond were in the doorway of her cottage when the Bentley pulled up.

"I'm not late Sally?" Cuthbert asked, opening the back doors.

"No, Raymond's been up half the night telling me all the taekwondo and boxing moves," Sally said.

"I think Mr Lumsden's going to have to watch his step where Raymond is concerned," Cuthbert said.

"Funny you should mention him, the ambulance driver called at the hotel this morning for coffee and he told me he picked up Lumsden the other day from the school. He's in a bad way after he fell in the showers. He broke his jaw and three ribs," she said.

"Sorry to hear that," Cuthbert smiled.

After a bowl of stilton and broccoli soup Raymond snapped everything that moved in the gardens and deer park.

"Take care with the camera, Raymond," Sally shouted.

"Sally, I want to take Raymond to the police labs as it could be where his future lies. The only thing is that his grandfather will be there," Cuthbert said.

"Yes, but dad doesn't know Raymond is his grandson, Go for it Cuthbert," Sally answered, patting his hand in a maternal way.

Chapter Twenty-Two

ON MONDAY MORNING CUTHBERT TURNED UP AT THE HOTEL HQ to find Bede busy setting up tables and chairs for the ten o' clock briefing. He was whistling some country and western tune and suddenly started to dance with one of the chairs.

"Good weekend George?" Cuthbert asked.

Bede turned with a grin as wide as Kemin Bay, "Thanks for the cottage sir, but it was a cold weekend as the heating was off. We had to sleep together to keep warm. We went to the Mull of Galloway lighthouse, had a great night at Port Logan Hotel, and even Jonathon said he enjoyed himself taking photographs with your old camera."

"You keep the key, George. Who knows, you might fancy another break. And by the way," Cuthbert went on, smiling, "I had the heating turned off when I gave you the key."

Dolly was busy catching up when Cuthbert walked in to her small office space. She gave him a look, a woman's look that showed she wasn't happy.

"I distinctly asked you not to question the men from the factory.

I made it clear in my report. The factory visit showed that they are not terrorists, they're just holding the fort for the real Mr Big. I can feel it, he's going to turn up very soon… I said surveillance only, not frighten them off!" Dolly spat.

"What if the 'Mr Big' were brothers?" Cuthbert asked.

"The Pevsner brothers?" She said without even thinking, "That would be some catch, they are ruthless killers."

"If the Arab and Somali know Hamilton, and they both know the Pevsners, does Hamilton also know the Pevsners? That would tie up a lot of loose ends," Cuthbert postulated.

"Did the Arab or Somali have anything to do with Patrick Dolan's death?" Dolly asked.

"No, the Arab said they had a big meeting with the brothers in Moscow, and I believe him. We are still no closer to finding Dolan's killer. What we do know though is that barmaid can't be Jinty Fergusson. I went to the school, the Headmistress told me Jinty actually died in a bush fire in Australia with her family. I think this girl is Domenica Hannah."

"Yes, when I ran the Judo club we went to The Girls' Institute in Glasgow and I'm sure it's the same girl. That scar on her cheek, that's why I remember her. But how do we prove it?" Dolly asked.

"I have a poem she wrote and signed at school. If I get her to write something now Dolly, with your skills in graphoanalysis, could you prove they were written by the same person?"

"*The sly fox jumped over the brown pig*, that would do it."

"Great."

Cuthbert thought Sunday morning would be a good time to take young Raymond Harris into Glasgow to meet Sam at the city's mortuary.

"Here he is Sam, the young boy who wants to follow in your footsteps, this is Raymond," Cuthbert introduced them.

"Where's the bodies?" Raymond asked, "On the television there are always bodies."

"The most important part of our job, Raymond, is cleaning: glassware, table tops and floors, everything must be hygienically clean," Big Sam replied, brushing off the question.

Sam took Raymond upstairs to see the particulates labs and Cuthbert left them to it, only returning a couple of hours later.

"Uncle Cuthbert! Sam took me upstairs and showed me the labs a real skeleton and took me for a burger!" Raymond said without taking a breath.

"I have a new book for you Raymond, it covers everything we talked about today. Who should I dedicate it to?"

"Harris, Raymond Harris. Can I come back again Sam?"

"Yes of course, but don't be disappointed if I have to suddenly leave or the lab has to be closed down because of a sudden death," Sam warned the young man, then turned to Cuthbert. "While you are here, I just completed Alan Broadsword's post-mortem."

"The Home Office chap found on the beach?"

"Yes, it was drowning, his lungs were full of foam but it was not straight forward," Sam scanned the report in his file, "He had enough legal highs in his system to kill an elephant."

"Broadsword had given a letter to the ferry steward with a Home Office address on it. In the letter Broadsword said he was tired of being blackmailed by Commander Hamilton and would never again run guns for him. Apparently Hamilton had found out he was a homosexual and was using underage rent boys," Cuthbert explained.

"He still had the keys for the van in his pocket," Sam noted.

Chapter Twenty-Three

CUTHBERT HAD TO GRAB THE DOOR OF THE BENTLEY AS HE TRIED to manhandle the huge bundle of books. The gust of wind was just a warning of what was to come according to the local fishermen.

"Hope you realise you've built up Carolyn's' hopes and dreams by giving so much praise to her?" Carolyn Jolly's mum Molly said.

"It's all well founded," Cuthbert reached out the four heavy books and she gestured that he bring them in.

"Scottish Criminal Law, Road Traffic Law, MacDonald's Establishing Precedents, Stated Cases on British Crime," Molly read the titles out loud.

"Informative but heavy, I thought I'd better drop them off for her," Cuthbert explained.

"She's just getting ready now as she's on the early shift," Mrs Jolly said.

"I'm on the early too, I'll take her in."

"It's true what they say about you," Molly said, "the Chief Inspector's caring but unbending." Jolly's head popped around the door frame, she was covered in a bath towel.

"I have made you a cuppa sir, and there are some biscuits this time," she said, smiling.

Cuthbert entered the station through the double doors and found Desk Sergeant Naylor busy on the radio.

"Problem Nat?" He asked.

"Sergeant Franks brought Victor Swan in last night and he is in cell two. After he had his breakfast he asked Sergeant Bede to feed his birds while Bede was up there doing a house search. Now George radios in to say the peahen attacked him when he went in to feed them."

"If it's a peahen they must be peacocks?" Cuthbert asked.

"Yes sir, but the hen laid an egg and became aggressive protecting it. Victor did warn him to be careful."

"Victor? On first name terms are we? He must have made an impression, but don't forget he may have strangled poor Paddy while he was sitting in the sun enjoying a pint."

"Yes sir, I will be more careful in future," Naylor said.

"Is George coming straight back Nat to do the interview with Swan?"

"Don't think so, he said he would call in the hospital for a couple of stitches as one of the cuts is close to the bone."

At that moment Sergeant Franks came in carrying a tray of hot teas. "Nat been telling you about the monster sir?" She asked.

"Just the person, Sergeant Franks, how would you like to sit in with me interviewing Swan?" Cuthbert asked.

"If you think I am up to it sir," Mary answered, "but when I informed him that he would be interviewed today, he said he had a right to remain silent as he had never met Paddy Dolan and he would say no comment to every question."

"We still have to follow procedure and give him the chance to answer," Cuthbert explained.

"Seems a waste of time," Mary countered.

"Anything come in last night Nat?"

"A Hughie Tuckerman called, he said he was passing the hotel at the time of the murder and had filled in a questionnaire but had heard nothing," Naylor answered,

"Did he leave a number to contact him?" Cuthbert asked.

"Said he worked at the council offices in Portpatrick, you can call any time and ask for the 'Bean Counter' he said."

"I will get over there now," Cuthbert informed them, "he might have seen our mystery man."

"Before I go Nat, I take it that after talking to Mary you know who the seven foot character was in the horror films?"

"Yes sir, it was the monster created by Doctor Frankenstein."

"Don't forget that Sergeant, it is usually used as a tiebreaker."

After twenty minutes in his office trying to work out how best to close down the factory in Well Road and catch Commander Hamilton and the Pevsner brothers at the same time with only one Inspector, Mary knocked and came in with a cup of tea. "You can't have Inspector Malone in two places at the same time," she said.

"Is my mind that easy to read Mary?" Cuthbert answered having a sip of tea, "Bede let us down failing the Inspector's examination."

"I would like to run the Well Road operation sir," Mary said, "I wouldn't let you down."

"Funny, I was thinking of that when you came in, but you are not even an acting Sergeant yet." Cuthbert said.

"So you might ask Jolly to do it now she's being promoted!" Mary spat.

"No way, it's you I want but I have changed the rota and I don't want you near Well Road. It's too dangerous and it is procedure."

"You will think about it though?" Mary asked and Cuthbert nodded.

Cuthbert was half way to Portpatrick when the radio hissed.

"Come in Nat, what have you got?"

"Paddy's van has turned up at Stranraer Breakers in Well Road, or what's left of it," Naylor said.

"Thank you Naylor, I'll get straight over there."

"Something else sir, Dolly says handwriting is one hundred per cent the same."

"Good," Cuthbert answered.

When Cuthbert turned up at the breakers the owner said it was just by chance that the van hadn't already been crushed. Jolly on a hunch had checked all the breakers. Cuthbert opened the only back door that was left on the van and sure enough found empty sacks with, 'Larne Animal Feed' printed on them.

"Something here sir," Sergeant Jolly shouted, trying to be heard over the car crusher.

"*Elephants are grey but not all grey things are elephants,*" Cuthbert read from the card Carolyn had found behind the sun visor.

"It was the front I thought you might find interesting sir."

Cuthbert turned the card over.

"Bearsden Exotic Birds, contact Victor Swan," Cuthbert read, "So what is the connection between Paddy and this Swan character?"

"He must have struggled with him while he was in the van because I have found his tie pin wedged between the seats," Sergeant Jolly lifted the shiny peacock tiepin.

Cuthbert finally arrived at Portpatrick Council Offices and was surprised at the young girl's response when he asked for Hughie Tuckerman, the Bean Counter. She had pressed the intercom and asked for the Troll to come down.

Cuthbert was stunned when he saw Tuckerman coming down the curved staircase. He was less than four feet in height but had a huge head and a stocky body.

"I am not a dwarf, people think I am but I am not," Tuckerman pointed out.

"There is no shame..." Cuthbert started.

"You are not listening Chief Inspector, read my lips, I have a disease called Diploid Triploid Mosaicism, I have three chromosomes in each cell as well as the usual two. I have a normal six foot body forced into a four foot frame."

"You informed my Desk Sergeant that you had information concerning the murder of Patrick Dolan," Cuthbert said.

"We can talk in here, it's what I call my escape hatch," he joked.

The room was the size of a broom cupboard without a window and had a table and one chair.

"What job you do here Mr Tuckerman?" Cuthbert asked.

"Please, call me Hughie. I check people's work to cut down on fraud and leaks."

"You must be the most hated person in the building," Cuthbert noted, to which Hughie just nodded. "Now you informed my Desk Sergeant you had some information regarding the murder of Patrick Dolan?"

"Although I didn't see this Irishman or the girl in question I did see two street girls standing next to the hotel and getting picked up by a man in a black Oxford Cambridge car."

"But if you didn't actually see anything of the murder..."

"Yes, but if you could trace the car driver or the two girls, they may have seen something," Hughie replied.

"Well yes, that would be possible. You said you had filled in a questionnaire, did you get the name of the officer?"

"Yes it was a Constable McKenzie, Barbie Campbell McKenzie," he said smugly.

Chapter Twenty-Four

WHILE ON HIS WAY TO THE DINING ROOM FOR THE FIVE THIRTY briefing Cuthbert noticed Sally struggling with a tray of crockery.

"Let me help you with that Sally," Cuthbert took the tray and put it on a worktop.

"Thank you Cuthbert, you have been very helpful recently," Sally said.

"I wonder if you would do something for me Sally?"

"What is it?"

"Can you keep me posted if Hamilton gets any visitors or starts acting differently?" "Course I can Cuthbert," Sally replied.

Bede and Dolly were busy in the Grand Hall, he was sorting out the seating while she was putting information packs on seats to taken away and digested. Dolly realised some people's brains are capable of absorbing information sporadically whereas for some it's like osmosis, it seeps in slowly. Cuthbert had noticed how Bede and Dolly had been working more in harmony, like two horses teamed up to pull together.

"I'm pleased to see you both working together now instead of against each other," he said.

"She's mellowed sir," Bede joked, "I think she's in love."

"George," Dolly joked, "keep it clean."

Just at that Seamus walked in carrying a massive bunch of flowers.

"She's in her office Seamus, just go through," Cuthbert pointed.

"It's you I wanted to see sir," Seamus answered. He didn't seem himself and was a bit shaky.

"Is Sean alright Seamus?" Cuthbert asked.

"Sean is fine now, he's started swimming and asked how far it is to Larne and back."

"Come in the bar Seamus, I've got half an hour before the briefing and I'll get you a drink," Cuthbert said.

"It's Dolly sir," Seamus started, "I've been seeing her quite a bit recently and I really like her."

"Do you love her?"

"Yes I do sir," Seamus answered, "and I know you're not her true father but I want your blessing for Dolly and me."

"She couldn't find a better man Seamus," Cuthbert said and toasted the union. "One thing you must realise, "he went on, "is when a woman finds love for her it is a temporary madness, a day without her man would be unthinkable, so be warned."

Cuthbert sat in the bar and watched Seamus leave. As he looked through the huge window to high above the harbour he saw the turbulent sky, jet black with streaks of red, peach and silver. It was mystical, like looking through a piece of coloured glass. A storm was brewing, he had heard the words a dozen times and he knew the morning would bring a conclusion and a number of arrests.

The great hall was a hub of excitement and commotion, Cuthbert clapped his hands loudly and silence fell.

"Well," Cuthbert started, "the sooner we get the briefing started the sooner we can all go home. I would like to thank each and every member of the team for not only the long hours but the amount of effort and detail you have put into the inquiry.

"Tomorrow arrests will be made, but let me make it clear: I don't want a lawyer or barrister finding some misdemeanour or cock up in procedure or a loophole for those arrested to escape through. If there is any small point you feel we should know about please inform Inspector Malone or myself."

"I would like to mention Constable Jolly. No instructions had been given to check local breaker's yards but Constable Jolly took it upon herself to do that. Well done Constable. Let that be an example to all of us, and not just senior ranks, to think about going that extra mile. It will be noted and acted upon. Now all I can say is again, thank you, and enjoy tonight."

Cuthbert had finally got his feet back on his own drive and was about to take the key out of the Bentley's ignition when the radio sounded. He wearily lifted the radio's receiver.

"What you got Nat?"

"It's Mary here sir, Sergeant Franks. Miss Hunter phoned from the school and said the groundsman, a Mr Potter, had detected a swarm of killer bees in a Chestnut tree at the school, she contacted the council but only got the answering service," Mary said.

"Had Nat ever heard of these killer bees, Mary?"

"I asked him and he left me an item printed in one of his comics from July this year. It said, 'Killer bees as far north as Durham: The killer bees that had crossed the channel last year and were seen in the Seven Oaks area of Kent were today seen swarming at Neville's Cross just outside of Durham. The bees originated from Northern Spain and are three times bigger than the British bee. The bees are lethal during their swarming period and their aggressive behaviour intensifies when they hear a droning sound, which they take as a threat to the Queen Bee'."

"Is Mr Potter waiting at the school for someone to attend?"

"Affirmative sir."

"Call her back, tell her I will attend personally. Fortunately I know somewhere to put these bees."

With the aid of a stick and a jar of honey he had managed to get the bees onto a sheet spread on the grass and then into a fine mesh bird cage. It was only when he was struggling to get the birdcage out of the Bentley back home that he realised it was wrong to put the killer bees into Anders Anderson's chalet. The bees could even kill the retired Dickinsons.

Chapter Twenty-Five

THE NEXT MORNING CUTHBERT WAS WOKEN BY THE SOUND OF A loud bang and deep moaning. The predicted storm had finally landed, which threatened to throw a very serious spanner into Cuthbert's works. He prayed the Larne to Stranraer ferry would not be cancelled. The phone rang; it was Dolly calling from the Larne Ferry Terminal.

"Good news sir, the targets have been seen boarding the ferry and it has just left."

He knew Dolly would have considered his worries and had phoned to put his mind at rest. It had been Dolly who insisted on receiving a full list of all passengers and vehicles on board the ferry before it had sailed. Patience, she knew, would be the key to the operation. Cuthbert rubbed his hands together, he loved watching a well organised plan unfolding.

A mini bus containing twelve Constables and a Sergeant followed a van containing dog handlers from the rear of Castlemilk Station bound for Well Road Industrial Estate in Stranraer. Nothing would be left to chance.

Hamilton had been out at first light to do checks on his Jaguar, the water, oil and he had even started the car's engine. His day was also prearranged.

The wind and rain pounded against Cuthbert's car windscreen as he made his way over to the station in Stranraer to pick up Bede. Naylor was alone at the desk when he arrived.

"You ever seen any killer bees?" Cuthbert asked.

"Only on film sir. Any problems at the school?"

Cuthbert shook his head.

"Dudgeon, that's a word that comes up at Biggar, Naylor."

"Medieval prison sir," Naylor replied.

"No that's dungeon," Cuthbert corrected, "Dudgeon means hilt, as on a knife, hence 'up to the hilt', and if there is a tie break don't rush in."

"Thank you sir," Naylor really appreciated all of his efforts, "I would love to win it."

Once Bede arrived they were quickly off heading out of the town. A huge black cloud was brought over the village by a fierce northerly and within seconds heavy raindrops were dancing off the Bentley's bonnet.

Sergeant Bede saw them first, two working girls dressed in Disney princess outfits, short and skimpy. The wind and rain were battering the two girls.

"Who would wear outfits like that? They disgust me," Bede snarled. "Even the tide would not take those two out."

"One day you will realise," Cuthbert pointed out, "that those girls on the streets are the eyes and ears of a modern police force."

He pulled the Bentley alongside them, got out and opened the back door. He could see them more clearly now, it was Bella and Aggie, two mature girls in their forties.

"A gentleman sir," Bella yelled, trying to make herself heard against the gale.

"I'll drop you both at the hotel and you can get some shelter and something hot to drink," Cuthbert said, handing them a small towel each.

"The Harbour Bar would be better, we can't get in the hotel," Aggie said.

"I am not surprised," Bede snorted.

"That's enough of that Sergeant," Cuthbert castigated him. "Show some respect, they do a job just like we do."

"You wouldn't believe the things that he shouts at us when he passes us in the street, it's disgusting."

"Well Aggie if it happens again," Cuthbert promised, "let me know and we will see how he likes walking the streets in this weather back on the beat in uniform. Tell me girls, were you two working last week? Last Friday night, at about half eight to half nine."

"Yes we were," Bella answered. "We were waiting beside the green at the side of the hotel. That's our pitch."

"We do a doubler on Fridays, he's a good tipper," Aggie added.

"Did you notice anything strange?" Cuthbert asked carefully. He didn't want to lead them.

"That's when the Irish lad was there sat on the bench, nice lad. He always waves," Bella noted.

"Yes and then that barmaid came out," Aggie now continued. "She must have known him really well."

"What makes you say that?" Cuthbert asked.

"She was friendly like, she put her arms around his neck like a cuddle and lifted him up, right up off the bench."

"What did he do after that Aggie?" Cuthbert went on, "Did he say anything?"

"No he just seemed to just slump to one side. We got our customer after that, our doubler.

That's when a customer wants…"

"That's enough," Cuthbert interrupted. "Here is a pound note for each of you, I will ask you both to give a statement in the near future, but for now get some hot soup and crusty bread off Frankie in the Harbour Bar. It's been a pleasure talking to you both."

"A gentleman sir," Aggie repeated, catching the side of Bede's face with her finger nail.

"That's for what you said about my father and him only been in the ground six weeks."

Bede winced and patted the drops of blood with a tissue, Cuthbert turned to him. "See the information we've picked up? It was just like Blackie Harris the chess master had described, the bluff then the double bluff. She does the second attack and rushes to tell us what she has done, by this we see she's a person with integrity who will own up to any crime she commits."

"She must have said a dozen times that she always owns up to something she has done," Bede added, "And we take her out of the equation when we look for the killer. Pretty clever stuff."

"Yes George," Cuthbert agreed. "Or maybe she was told the plan while on remand by an inmate in Carstairs Mental Institute."

"What about this Victor Swan sir? Did he have any part in this?" Bede asked.

"I think when she bumped into him she meant to bump into him, she was looking for a fall guy."

"She staged the whole thing, planting the swan in the Bridal Suite and fitting the lens cap over the camera on the back stairs. She had access to those areas because she worked at the hotel."

"What about the card and the tie pin in Paddy's van," Bede asked.

"Paddy had been to the hotel many times before and she would have known where he parked it," Cuthbert explained.

"I wonder why Swan won't tell us where he was that Friday night? His alibi would clear him."

"Maybe he was doing something embarrassing. I hope that diary you found at his house can reveal his whereabouts."

Just then the radio crackled, "Come in Nat," Cuthbert said.

"Dolly just radioed from the ferry and said the Pevsners had boarded the ferry as foot passengers with no car. She thinks Hamilton may drive up to Stranraer to pick them up. Whatever he is selling to them must be small enough to fit into a suitcase."

"Radio her back, Nat, tell her Hamilton is leaving now so her assumption seems correct. We will follow him at a safe distance."

"Another thing sir, Captain Jack the Harbour Master radioed to say he was shadowing a Russian trawler anchored off Kemin Bay Head."

"See if he can pull it in on some technicality, that must be the Pevsners escape route."

Cuthbert fired up the Bentley and headed north toward the Ferry Terminal.

"So the brothers might not be going to the arms factory?" Bede asked.

"Mary is running the Well Street side of the mission and she phoned last night to say a twin wheeled truck was parked outside the factory door. Sean said he would take his truck up there this morning to block the exit road from the estate when Mary gives the nod."

"You are putting a lot of trust in Mary sir, is she qualified to run the operation?" "Technically no. I expected Dolly to follow the brothers from Belfast to the factory but the plans seem to have changed."

"If Hamilton does the exchange with the brothers at Kemin Bay Head, how will they get from the headland on the cliffs down to the beach?"

"Yes I was thinking that George, get the map from the glove compartment and see if there's any way down."

"Port Logan sir, they could bring a small boat alongside the jetty and pick them up there," Bede pointed.

"Good thinking George, well done."

Nat's voice came over the airways once more, "Captain Jack has detained the trawler sir, he's towing it up to the police marine craft centre in Gairloch on a charge of piracy. And another thing, Mary radioed to say the police dogs were making a hell of a racket as the factory unit they are using is supposedly closed down. Should she stand the dog unit down?"

"Tell her it is her show and she must decide," answered Cuthbert, "but remind her she will need the team after the operation has been completed. She'll need the sniffer dogs to determine if any other terrorist equipment has been hidden."

Chapter Twenty-Six

MARY SAT IN THE PASSENGER'S SEAT OF THE POLICE MINIVAN WITH Sergeant Jolly beside her in the driver's seat, waiting for the Police Operations Team to arrive. They were made up of a team of newly trained constables being led by Sergeant Price, a team of highly trained sniffer dog handlers based at Castlemilk, and an Armed Response Unit from Durham. Mary had done the preliminary work, instructing Sergeant Price to radio when they left and also if there was any problems on route. She had also met Seamus on his arrival at the estate and thanked him for his help, saying she knew she could rely on him to close off the exit before they moved in.

She hoped Sergeant Price would act in a professional manner, not only was he a 'Copper's Copper' respected by officers of all ranks but many spoke highly of his abilities. His operations experience far outweighed his Sergeant's stripes.

Mary opened the neighbouring factory's back door and with Seamus's help managed to get the big portable space heaters running. She put on the water boiler and put the milk bottles into the small refrigerator. A small convoy of vehicles pulled into the parking area and she went out to meet them. She realised it would be a long day for the government officials.

"A message from the Chief Inspector," Carolyn Jolly read from her pocket book. "You run the show but remember, when the factory workers have been removed, assessed and shipped out, you will need the dog handlers to check for hidden bomb making materials."

Mary decided now was the time to move in and asked all the team to assemble around two fold away decorator's tables. "Before we go in," she started, "I want every person to be on first name terms with the two sets of plans of the factory layout. This one is the first floor and this one of the ground floor," she pointed. She remembered Dolly's words – 'Keep it simple but professional'. Inspector Malone had said she was proud of Mary volunteering for such a technically difficult and potentially dangerous operation.

Mary met the officials in turn as they arrived: Shirley from the people trafficking unit, Johnson from Works and Pensions, and finally Smyth from the terrorist intelligence unit. She assured them that everyone to be interviewed would be brought to the unit, searched for weapons and scanned for explosive or radioactive particles before being brought over.

Mary knew she would find it difficult to show them that she was in charge and understood their need for reassurance that no one was going to be injured in the operation, especially with them knowing that bomb making equipment was on site.

"Can I have your attention," she shouted, "I want to clarify three main points before we go in. Firstly, it is an old factory so safety is of paramount importance. Stick to the two main rooms on the ground floor with team A at the back driving all the workers to the front clockwise. Team B, your task will be to open the main loading door and move in an anti-clockwise direction, checking all rooms are clear and finally meeting up with the other team.

"Secondly, when you come into contact with the workers make it clear to them that you are leading them to safety and not arresting them. Most of the workers will be refugees who have paid the people in charge to take them to a better life and not to end up confined to a factory working as slaves.

Now lastly, a part of the factory is cordoned off with black and yellow tape as it is unsafe, please keep clear of this area. More than anything you're here to get these people out of the factory, searched, scanned for harmful particles and then put onto a bus. Although everything in the factory is lethal nothing is primed and ready for action, the bomb equipment is not assembled and without detonators. Be more wary of hypodermics than knives and arrest using minimal force."

The factory was set back from the others, as if in hiding. On one side was open derelict land covered in brambles and litter, while on the other side was an ideal staging point with builder's skips and packs of bricks and blocks giving good cover and room to pass freely.

The front of the building showed little change from when it had been constructed, though the paintwork on its doors and windows was blistered and chipped. A new sign had been recently fixed above the arched doorway read 'Valspar Batteries'.

Both doors had been fastened back to the wall giving them access to a turban headed forklift driver who was bringing pallets from the factory and loading a large truck.

Mary's throat was dry and she had no sweat on her hands as she led the first assault team to the back. There was access through a courtyard with a rusted fire escape that lead to three balconies on the upper floor and a metal fire escape door at its far end. She flattened herself against the brickwork as the armed unit moved into position, their weapons pointed downwards. They were followed up the stairs by a team of constables. They waited for the signal from Mary, who put a whistle to her mouth but waited. She heard the Sergeant getting his team into position at the front on either side of the front doorway.

Mary ran to the top of the stairs, caught her breath, and waved to Seamus to block the exit way. The armed officers watched her every move, their fingers tight on the trigger guards, knowing synchronization was the heartbeat of the whole operation.

After the two heavily built officers passed her and were in front of the emergency exit Mary blew the whistle.

The team at the front simply walked in through the open door and found the workers to be foreign immigrants, only too glad to be rescued from their imprisonment. The Arab and Somali were nowhere to be seen. The voices on the stairs were loud and clear, "Stop what you are doing and go to the front entrance."

Within ten minutes of sending in the dogs the factory was deemed safe and Constable Mary Franks breathed a sigh of relief.

Chapter Twenty-Seven

CUTHBERT DROVE ALONG THE SEAFRONT WITH BEDE IN THE FRONT passenger seat looking right and left for Hamilton's Jaguar. Dolly sat in the back looking into the boot area, something was bothering her.

"You got something in the back here," she said, "it sounds like buzzing…"

"Killer bees," Cuthbert informed her. "They're in a birdcage, I forgot all about them."

"There's Hamilton's car parked on the beach beside the lobster pots sir," Bede said.

"No way will I go onto the sand with the tide coming in," Cuthbert assured them. He parked on the coast road and asked Bede to bring the birdcage and for Dolly to stay in the car. As he got closer to Hamilton he saw he was standing at the back of his car handing the Pevsners a large envelope and in return for a small case.

"I seem to have the balance tipped in my favour Chief Inspector," Hamilton started. "You have justice on your side while I have this Colt Taurus," he pointed the Taurus at Cuthbert's chest. "Keep back until we do our transaction then we will be long gone."

"So what is it Hamilton? Something small enough to fit into an envelope. Information or plans?"

"I said keep back, or I will fire," Hamilton yelled as the wind suddenly became stronger and turned into an easterly.

"Aim for the heart, isn't that your motto? You're jealous of people who have one."

"I warned you," Hamilton fired five bullets into Cuthbert's chest and the force of the volley knocked him onto his back. He looked over to the Bentley to see Bede running along the sand to join him and Dolly getting out of the car holding her Colt Python. Bede dropped the birdcage at Cuthbert's feet and was met by Hamilton's stare.

"You keep back sonny or you will get the same as your governor."

Bede kept on walking and when Hamilton tried to fire the chamber was empty.

"That is the trouble with the Taurus," Cuthbert said, standing tall and opening his coat to reveal the kevlar bulletproof vest.

A deep humming ship's horn sounded and their heads turned to see Captain Jack's Harbour cutter towing the Russian trawler. Dolly joined them.

"You're coming with us Hamilton," Dolly shouted.

"No, I think we should make him an offer," Cuthbert said. "Hand over the envelope and case and you can get in the car with your friends and go as far as you can."

Hamilton threw the envelope at Cuthbert and waved the Pevsner brothers to join him, they watched in horror as their car wheels spun, now surrounded by seawater. Cuthbert walked over to the Jaguar, lifted the boot hatch and hurled the birdcage into the car, breaking the bamboo structure in half. Within seconds the three men's faces were covered in killer bees, even more excited now after hearing another drone from the captain's horn. As the water was just about to fully submerge the car they watched the bees swarm above it and then fly off east.

"Wonder where they're headed?" Dolly asked.

"Neville's Cross near Durham, to a battle site against other killer bees," Cuthbert said smiling.

As they looked out there was nothing to see, only the cry of the gulls and the roar of the incoming waves crashing against the pier.

Chapter Twenty-Eight

CUTHBERT RAN OVER TO MARY AND HUGGED HER WHEN HE arrived at Well Road Industrial Estate. "What did I say about keeping out of the way and letting the others do the dangerous stuff!"

"I did what you would have done and led from the front," Mary answered.

"Well there is a promotion coming your way. After today I personally think you will go right to the top."

"Thank you sir."

"But always remember, it takes a lifetime to build a reputation and only seconds to ruin it," Cuthbert said.

He was pleased the vans holding the Glasgow police hadn't left. He put a case of Arran special into each van. "Is there a Constable Campbell McKenzie here?" He asked.

A tall blonde girl stood to a round of applause, she was wearing civilian clothes and her hair was wet. Cuthbert led her to the factory's upstairs rest area, passing a dog handler coming down who told them the upstairs was clear. Cuthbert pointed to a chair opposite and they sat down.

"Barbie Campbell McKenzie," he read from the Police Disciplinary Form. "Are you new Barbie?"

"I haven't been unwrapped yet sir, I got top grades at the Police Training College," she answered, slowly taking off her white Versace jacket. She was wearing a tangerine cut off t-shirt with two small pearl buttons at the top and an *I Love NY* slogan on the front, a matching short tennis skirt and a Miami Dolphins peaked cap. Cuthbert's eyes were riveted to her massive breasts.

"Very nice," he commented.

"They were a birthday present, buy one get one free," she answered, putting the palm of her hand under each breast and wobbling them.

"No, I meant getting the top grades was very nice. Does your mother not mind?" He asked.

"She paid for them," she said, smiling. "Mother was on the stage under the name of Sylvia Simms."

"So you have done a bit of marching over the last month?" He asked and she nodded. "Well let's see you march, see how good you are."

Barbie sauntered across the room with a dazzlingly lascivious walk. The policeman's eyes were glued to her hips and as they swayed he watched her short skirt ride up to reveal her pants.

"Do you get excited watching my body Chief Inspector?" She asked.

"No," Cuthbert lied, getting very excited. "You are a smart girl Barbie, have you ever thought of being part of the designer fashion industry?"

"I am part of the industry, as a photographer," she pulled a small wallet from her bag and took out a photograph, "Do you recognise that?"

"God... that's George Bede pulling a girl out of the sea on Portpatrick Beach."

"Notice her blonde tangled hair spread over her grey puffy cheeks, and the way he wrapped his arms around her breasts to keep them covered from the gawkers. That photograph I took spelled out panic and pity. I got five pounds for the picture from the Glasgow Herald but after it went global it got me a job on the New York Times.

"I turned up at crime scenes to take pictures of things I couldn't normally look at. I felt safe looking at them through a lens. My sanctuary was my dark room and my peace was looking through each film knowing I had frozen a part of history," she said.

"You want to give up that for Strathclyde Police?"

"That was just a job, I want a career. I hope I don't have anything to spoil that."

Cuthbert found his eyes being drawn to her chest, she caught him and he turned away embarrassed, studying the tops of his shoes.

"Is your hair natural?" He asked.

"Yes, it naturally comes out of a bottle," she answered.

She pulled a pair of expensive sunglasses from her bag and put them on and then smoothed her hair down in an elegant movement.

"Nice lenses," he commented.

"Beverley Hills, Rodeo Drive," she said. "Some Arab Prince was getting married last week and wanted me to do the shoot. He offered me a blank cheque. I turned him down to complete my training, but he is coming to Glasgow this weekend to do the shoot with his new wife at the People's Palace. I will be staying at the Portpatrick Hotel. Maybe now's the time I should be getting unwrapped. I feel a little bit frightened, it will be my first time," she whispered.

"You think you have found the man to do that?"

"I don't *think* I have found him I *definitely know*," she undid the two pearl buttons and leaned over to pick up Cuthbert's pen. She wrote something on the Police Disciplinary Form, folded it, and put it in the top pocket of his coat.

"Why not come up and see me Big Man?" She pulled on her jacket and headed for a mirror to check her appearance. She then swayed to the top of the stairs, turned her head quickly and caught him watching her. She stopped and slowly lifted her finger and shook it. Cuthbert smiled.

Chapter Twenty-Nine

DOLLY HAD SPENT THE WHOLE DAY TRYING TO DECODE VICTOR Swan's diary but was stumped on five or six words after going through every code in the book. She was joined by Cuthbert, Bede, Mary and Carolyn to try to work out the words.

As Dolly read them out they could hear laughing, it was Desk Sergeant Nathanial Naylor bringing in Victor.

"Come on Nat you must know what a 'Double Whammy', 'Jitterbugs', 'Hula Poppers' and 'River Runts' are," she asked.

"They are all lures used by fishermen," Victor told them.

"Now that you are talking Victor, can you tell me if I have decoded this correctly?" Dolly asked, and he nodded. "You joined the Bearsden Bird Breeders Club where you met fishermen Harold and Marti from Harris. Were they brothers?"

Victor shook his head.

"The ferry service confirmed that you sailed to Harris on the afternoon Patrick Dolan was murdered, so you had an alibi and you could have cleared yourself straight away…"

"Were you sleeping with Harold and felt embarrassed?" Carolyn interrupted,

"No." Victor answered quietly.

"Where you sleeping with Marti while Harold went night fishing?" Mary asked.

Victor nodded.

"So Marti goes out fishing…" Mary pressed on.

"Marti is frightened of the water," Victor said.

"So if Marti doesn't go fishing what does she enjoy doing?" Mary asked.

"What she enjoys doing got her pregnant and her husband Harold is impotent," Victor sobbed.

"You think he is cheeky and disrespectful?" Cuthbert asked.

"No, he just can't get it up with Marti. He will know it's not his baby," Victor explained.

Cuthbert brought a bottle of Cognac from his drawer and Naylor brought a tray of glasses from a side table.

"Will you join us Victor, now that you are free to go home to your birds? I just hope this egg the peahen is protecting is worth all the trouble," Cuthbert said and Victor nodded.

"This Cognac was first drunk by Napoleon at his coronation in 1802."

Everyone toasted Victor and then Cuthbert stood up, "Now that we know that this girl is solely responsible for poor Paddy's death, I insist you all take extra care over the next few days. I don't want her claiming Police brutality. You will all work in pairs, with no exceptions." He insisted.

George Bede wandered out to the car and was quickly followed by Dolly.

"You heard what Cuthbert said, we work in pairs, so no sneaking off. Make sure you have plenty of petrol in that car. I don't want to be coming out to you again with a can of petrol like last night."

Bede shook the empty petrol can and waited for her to go back inside. He thought about going to the toilet before he left but shook his head and fired up the Thunderbird

As he looked down at the car's fuel gauge he saw Domenica entering the car park of the Portpatrick Hotel carrying a bunch of flowers. He pulled into the car park then slowly approached her in the Japanese Garden.

"You come with me, you're going for a short ride," Bede said, holding her arm.

"I brought some flowers for poor Paddy, did you arrest the monster that killed him?" She asked.

"He is at the police station as I speak," Bede lied. "We need you to formally identify him." Bede looked down at her hands, which were covered in black paint. He quickly took a car blanket from the boot and spread it on the back seat. Once she was inside the car Bede snapped the handcuffs on her wrist and to an armrest. She started banging her head against the front seat.

"I will say that you beat me," she said.

Suddenly Diep approached the car and pointed her camera into Domenica's face.

"You can say what you want, but the camera never lies," Diep said.

Domenica grabbed the petrol can, started to unscrew the top and took her lighter from her pocket.

"Don't even think about it…" Bede warned.

"What, you don't want me to damage the car like I did the last one?"

She started pouring the can's contents over her head and then stopped and smelled the can.

"You dirty pig!" She shouted.

"I'm sorry, I was going for petrol and I needed the toilet," Bede explained.

He contacted Cuthbert and told him the situation. Cuthbert said the answer to the murder had just landed and he was on his way.

Bede was confused when he saw Cuthbert carrying two pairs of gardening gloves.

"We will lift these black metal railings one at a time and inspect them," Cuthbert said.

Although not a hot day the sun was very bright and after five or six minutes of moving the railings he asked Bede to stop. Beneath a second pile of railings he saw something shining in the sun's rays. He pulled a pen from his pocket and looped the small hospital bracelet from the point of the piece of short railing and slipped it into an evidence bag.

"There are two names on the bracelet George," he said.

"I can see *Carstairs Mental Institute*," Bede read.

"The other says *The Urban Chameleon*," Cuthbert said, "and if I am not mistaken that looks like blood."

"So she saw the shorter piece of metal lying when she was planning Paddy's murder," Bede said.

"Yes, but didn't expect to lose her hospital bracelet on the actual railing. That is what she came here to look for after she found the camera lens cap she had hidden."

Chapter Thirty

"THE BIGGAR ARTS, CRAFTS AND AMATEUR PHOTOGRAPHY SHOW," read the banner which stretched over the front door way of the entrance. The subtitle read, "London's Big, but Biggar's, Biggar." One of Mary Franks' little jokes. Constable Franks had been a real revelation on the show committee, helping volunteers and fund raisers. They were impressed with her and her catch phrase, "Young blood sharing old traditions, where young enthusiasts are schooled by the experienced."

To open the show Father Brown came forward to welcome all and thank everyone for coming. The Glasgow girl's school gave a rendition of the Skye Boat song, and as the song ended a large wind machine started up and the room faded into total darkness. A spotlight picked up Sean, dressed as Moses with robes and a long walking pole, who started singing:

When Israel was in Egypt's land
Let my people go
Oppressed so hard they could not stand
Let my people go

Go down, Moses, right down to Egypt's land
Tell old Pharaoh
Let my people go

Big Sam now came onto the stage and applause rang out. The ten contestants who had entered the General Knowledge Quiz followed him on stage. Cuthbert caught Naylor's arm as he passed.

"Good luck Nat," he said.

"Thank you sir," Naylor smiled.

"Simultaneously we will have a demonstration of Judo from Dorothy Malone and young Raymond Harris," Sam announced. Raymond's proud mum Sally strode up and took a photograph

"We also have a boxing exhibition featuring Seamus O' Connell and Chief Inspector Cuthbert Durham." Sam went on.

When Naylor turned over the question paper his hand was shaking. He quickly scanned the first few questions: "two kestrels," "a dudgeon" and "which animal from South America." His hand quickly stopped shaking and he smiled.

"Thank you for the demonstrations. Now the result of the quiz and it's a tie between Mr Jack McDuff and Nathanial Naylor! So the first to raise a hand and answer will be the winner." Mary Franks handed the Father the tie breaker question.

"In the Hammer House of Horror films, what name was given to the seven foot monster with a bolt?"

McDuff's hand hit the ceiling, "Frankenstein!" He yelled, lifting both arms into the air.

"That answer is incorrect, can you answer Nathanial?"

"The answer is the monster. Doctor Frankenstein created the monster."

"That answer is correct, meaning a new winner of the General Knowledge Gold Cup. Nathanial Naylor, congratulations, please come forward to receive the cup."

Mary Franks had trouble restraining her emotions but she knew that as a Judge she had to be impartial.

"The next competition, the water colour, has only one winner, although the standards were very high. The winner is Flora MacDonald, with her water colour, The Portpatrick Belle. Please come forward to receive the shield."

Cuthbert stood up applauded, the tears rolling down his cheeks.

"Well done Flora," said Father Brown again. "The Glasgow girl's school choir will now sing The Shepherd Song."

As the song slowly ended the sound of thunder rang out and red lights flashed on and off. Then Naylor, dressed as the Devil, started: "By ye Gods of Satan, for vengeance is mine see the lord as I sit at the right hand of the dark side."

Then on the opposite side of the stage Seamus, dressed as Captain Blyth, began, "Bring her into the wind Fletcher Christian and I'll keel hall any man to within an inch of his life if my orders aren't followed."

Big Sam came onto the stage.

"Our first competitor in the poetry competition is introduced by his granddaughter, Lucy Alexandria."

"Can you please put your hands together for my grandfather China, with his own composition, *War veterans stand as carved from stone*."

China came onto the stage in a wheelchair with a small oxygen bottle at his feet and a mask tied around his neck. He began to read his poem.

War veterans stand as carved from stone
They play a waiting game, a losing hand
Apostle talks in a different tongue
Flaming heads a mitre of a promised land

Past faces drawn in lines on marbled stone
Worn by tide from autumn wind's breath
Helmets hung over bayonets fixed
Sun going down announces another comrade's death

Death shroud knows not the burial plot
Yet follows the raven's cry
Mourning mission bell lost in time
Waits for the obituary sigh

Drummer boy beats a marching pace
Buglers sound reveille slow
Flag bearer carries the colours with pride
Romantic full moon brings memory heart glow

Pointer long counts down an ending
Sand in glass a measured falling
Calendar depicts the same picture
Wait the last order the final calling

Lucy Alexandria pushed China from the stage to applause while Big Sam Harris again came up on to the stage.

"Two of my own staff, Polly Anna and Pandora, will now sing, Sisters."

After the song Big Sam re-appeared, "Next we have the photography competition. In second place with Yellow Hammer on Midnight Emerald, please come forward, George Bede, and receive the silver cup. For the first time we have a dead heat for the Gold Cup, a new one has been purchased for the first winner, young Jonathon Bede, with "Hamster brothers playing piggy back." Well done Jonathon, please come forward!

"I now have the very great honour to announce the other co-winner," McDuff got to his feet in anticipation of making his way to the stage. "The winner is Raymond Harris for 'Stag at Dunsky Castle'. Come up Raymond."

McDuff turned to get back to his seat only to find a huge pair of bloomers spread across his chair.

The girls from Dundee, Cuthbert thought, *up to their tricks*.

Big Sam Harris handed Raymond the trophy, his mum stood and took a photograph then all three huddled together.

Mary Franks now entered the stage, "The home-made cake competition, winner Morag Franks, please come forward."

Cuthbert leaned over to catch Morag as she passed with a huge glass dish.

"What is the secret ingredient Morag?" He asked.

"A herb," she smiled, "called marijuana."

The next event was the amateur poetry competition. Poppy, a young schoolgirl with a huge smiling sun on her t-shirt, read her work *Searching* from her blue school exercise book.

My love can speak rhymes and beautiful verse
He always knows that which I seek
And through his glimpse how the world should be
closeness to God and peace eternally
But the absolute truth is elusive to me

I walk through the fields and see the clean river
Where sorrows vanish with the wind and the weather
And oneness with nature is balm to the soul
Is this the secret or is God my goal

Darling you can't tell me the secret that you hold
It is a gift from the angels never to be told
And so I'll go on searching the hills, the woods and sea
Until some day your angels perhaps, may smile on me

There could be only one winner, and Cuthbert handed Poppy the huge Gold Cup and hugged her.

"Now the final event for Best Performer," Father Brown said.

Lisa Bede came on stage and sang a version of "Wind beneath My Wings." Mary Franks handed Bede the Silver Salver. "Give it to Lisa, George, she deserves it."

He went up smiling with Jonathon and gave it to her and they all hugged together, a happy, contented family. Cuthbert sat back and took a deep breath, everything was over and he could relax. Nothing could spoil the day.

At that he heard loud screaming and found the Father lying on the foyer floor with Poppy beside him. He put his arm around her to console her. His face was close to hers and he whispered, "It's alright he's just fallen over."

A flash of light then hit the foyer like a streak of lightning.

"Fallen over like hell," Father Brown yelled. "Someone hit me over the head with a pair of binoculars."

"The man took a photograph," Poppy sobbed, "that was the light."

Cuthbert sat Poppy down beside him and tried to console her with Dolly bringing her a glass of orange juice.

"You have gone from a drab duckling to a radiant swan Poppy," he said. "I will take you home in the Bentley." Poppy's smile was wide.

Cuthbert sighed, "I thought nothing could spoil today."

Suddenly Sergeant Jolly was standing in front of him.

"Carolyn, I thought you were on desk duty?" Cuthbert asked, "It's not your mother?"

"No sir," Jolly answered. "The body of an elderly man has been pulled out of Portpatrick Harbour. It's Ahab. Killed himself by the look of it."

Cuthbert sat Carolyn Jolly down and went over to give the news to Flora, Ahab's wife. She let out a shriek and Margo hugged her to console her.

"I had better stay with her tonight Cuthbert, she will need me," she said, and Cuthbert nodded.

Driving Poppy home Cuthbert stopped at a viewing point at Witch's Cove. They both looked out into the darkness with only the light from a thousand stars.

"This could be the start of a new world for you Poppy, but there is one thing I want you to promise me: never go to the Celtic stone on the moor alone. I have been having these dreams about you… well, just stay off the moor."

"You really worry about me," she smiled, and leaned over and kissed him.

Cuthbert saw another flash of light and got out of the car but whosoever shadow he had seen in the rear window was now long gone.

"I haven't got you into trouble?" Poppy asked.

"No, but I had best get you home as the fishermen are saying we may have thunder tonight."

Cuthbert had only got half way back to his cottage when he saw the fork of lighting followed shortly after by the huge clap of thunder. In the distance he could see his cottage roof glowing a bright orange colour, flames shooting high into the sky. It was only when he pulled into his drive that he saw it was Anders Anderson's chalet that was on fire. It was the oil from the pine that had given off the strange glow effect.

Cuthbert sat in the Japanese Garden looking at the seat poor Paddy had sat on. Fate had brought him to meet the evil which had taken his life. He felt inside his coat pocket and took out Barbie's Discipline Action Form and read the words she had written over her charge of acting in an unprofessional manner: "No further action, the girl needs to be educated by someone in control. She needs to be unwrapped and has been waiting for the right person, P. P. Hotel after ten, room Thirty- Three."

He saw her stood in the doorway when he came out of the lift, the silk nightshirt she wore barley covered her yellow panties that he had noticed when she reached for her nightgown.

He did a pitiful job trying not to stare.

Next morning it was Barbie's huge false eyelashes he tried to focus on but her face was already made up with indigo eye shadow and some orange brown cream on her skin.

"So you're finally with us Big Man," she said smiling. "I thought you might unwrap me again, it's funny I waited all this time to do it and now I know how much I enjoy it, maybe I should have tried it earlier."

Cuthbert rolled her over onto her own pillar and saw her more clearly. She was totally naked apart from a Disney World tank top and Pluto ears.

"I was thinking about what you were saying last night, about coming to Stranraer Police Station. I think your future lies with photography and you should go back to The New York Times. I have a thousand to get you back on your feet."

"Alright Big Man, but I will miss you," she smiled. "Now, will you unwrap me?"

"Give me five minutes to shower, it may have been your first time but I lost count after that." As Cuthbert walked away she raised her little finger into the air.

Another sucker wrapped around my little finger, another mug thought he had taken me for the first time. Some Big Man, more like Big Wanktoid in the little ghost town of your little world. Yes I am off to the Big Apple, with or without your say so. Men are all like little children to use and then leave, she thought.

Cuthbert came back showered and fresh as the Midnight Cowboy.

"Steady on cowboy," Barbie said, getting up and opening her waterproof aluminium camera carrier. She clipped a six hundred millimetre lens on the Nikon camera and slid in a black and white film. She preferred to work in black and white, it gave a more dramatic, gritty look.

"What you think of the cap I had tailor made for you?" She asked.

The hat was a black sailor's cap with a long peak and a white mesh that lay at the back of the neck to avoid sunburn. She held up the cap to show him the lettering above the peak.

"I just want one personal picture I can look at anywhere in the whole world and say that I had a night with the Big Man. I don't think you realise what that means to me."

Cuthbert could feel his face redden.

"I like the fancy pink lettering saying *the big man*," Cuthbert said, "but what is the white mesh for?"

She quickly slipped the cap over his head and pulled down the mesh over his neck, at the back. "It is to stop your neck getting sunburnt," she lied. She didn't tell him it was to cover the upper letters that were visible now that the mesh had been removed.

Her forefinger squeezed the shutter button while her thumb levered the rewind, within minutes she had snapped a full set.

"These will give you plenty of pleasure," Cuthbert boasted.

"Cuthbert, I can honestly say you won't believe the pleasure these pictures will give me," Barbie said, grinning.

Desk Sergeant Naylor was still in shock and needed to keep looking at the eight by six add in the personal column of the previous night's Glasgow Herald to remind himself he was not dreaming. The Chief Inspector was pictured sitting up on a bed naked apart from a white sailor's cap. The wording on the cap read, *Looking for the Big Man*, while the wording beneath the photograph read, *Boy in blue in Stranraer looking for big man, big and black*.

On the Sunday morning it was Chief Inspector Cuthbert Durham who didn't like Sundays. It wasn't raining but he knew that Desk Sergeant would be gloating after his win in the Biggar show.

"Postcard came in for you, from Harris sir," Naylor said, looking strangely at Cuthbert.

"You alright Nat?" Cuthbert asked and Naylor nodded. "What does Victor say in his postcard?"

"I wouldn't think of reading your mail sir."

"And?" Cuthbert prompted.

"Harold is over the moon about Marti being pregnant and they are going to live together all three of them."

"And?" Cuthbert waited.

"The one egg under the peahen that had not hatched turned out to be made of pottery, another one of the Urban Chameleon's little jokes."

Cuthbert went into his office and started filling in the overtime sheets. He looked up to see Naylor standing in the doorway.

"Spit it out Sergeant, what is it?" Cuthbert asked.

"This advert in last night's Glasgow Herald sir," Naylor said, "in the Personal Ads…"

"Are you interested then Nat?"

Naylor turned away, embarrassed, "I like you and respect you sir, but not like that."

"You have lost me Nat, why were you looking in the Personal Ads?"

Naylor spread the newspaper over Cuthbert's desk, "That is the personal ad sir," he pointed.

"Bloody Nora!" Cuthbert shouted, "Who has put that in the paper!"

They both looked up as a dark shadow stood in the doorway. He was black, over seven feet tall and built like a Quarterback, "Hi cutie, my name is Leroy, but the boys at the Blue Oyster Bar call me Horse, the Dark Horse."

"Bloody Constable Barbie Campbell McKenzie," Cuthbert groaned.

"It takes a lifetime to build a reputation and one moment to ruin it."

What happens next?

Read the next episode in the continuing story of the people in the Scottish village…

THE BONE BIBLE

New Year's Eve was a time for the villagers to reflect, to look back. The savage murder of Irishman Patrick Dolan, Paddy, had opened a deep wound that would carry a lasting scar.

News of the retirement of Father Valentine filtered through to the isolated cottages; the fact he was being replaced by a women would take people time to come to terms with.

Each villager had said an extra prayer for peace to return but when winter turned to spring, school children started to go missing. With no children being found and little sign of progress the villagers began to question whether the Chief Inspector Cuthbert Durham was up to the challenge…

The Bone Bible

Introduction

POPPY SAT BACK AND TOOK IN THE STRONG AROMAS OF THE heath and heather, enjoying the late afternoon sunshine. She relished the coldness on her back, seeping from the huge hand carved Celtic stone on the Scottish moor. The pagans' primitive tools had scribed the image thousands of years earlier. As she pressed her finger into the inscription of the snake biting its own tail she closed her eyes and tried to remember the meaning of the emblem.

The Ouroboros was the ancient Greek symbol, depicting the future and not the past, of Divine life that embraced cyclical systems, unity, evolution, birth and death.

Poppy had endured a long last day before the summer break at the Portpatrick School and now contemplated starting a new term at her new school in Stranraer.

She unfastened the buttons on her white blouse and thought of the rules she had broken in being on the moor.

Not going straight home, she knew her mum would be wondering where she was and if she was getting her school uniform dirty. Her dad would be going mad if he knew she was wasting her time writing poetry instead of concentrating on her school work.

Then the nice policeman, Cuthbert, had taken her home after the Biggar Show because she was upset about the scuffle in the foyer. She knew the real reason why he took her home was because he loved her, the same way she loved him. He was a lot older than her but he hadn't complained when she had kissed him on the cheek at the viewing area near to where she lived on the edge of the moor. 'Promise me you will never go to the Celtic Stone alone', he had warned, but 'rules are made to be broken' is what Miss Hunter had said at school.

Poppy laid her school work book on the grass and rubbed her finger over the small red heart she had drawn. Cuthbert, the policeman had laughed when he had seen her real name in the margin.

'Ruth? Is that just your Sunday school name?' he had teased.

She held both her hands up in front of her face, looking through her puffy white skin, bright pink in the big golden sun's rays. Suddenly it went dark, pitch dark and a horrible smell of dry oats and sacking made her start to cough. She started to kick out her legs and struggle against the person picking her up.

Poppy could not prevent being carried away; he was too strong. Maybe she would not be starting the new school after the holidays after all.

It was still dark without an ounce of breathe and only the faintest sound coming from the birds and farm animals in the near distance. Andre Lazarus Moussa hadn't slept, for every time he had closed his eyes her young bloodied face, covered in her long flowing hair had appeared, unmoving, not breathing but asking over and over again, like a rabbi's mantra, 'why me, why me?'

Closing his eyes and trying to forget her only made him see the faces of the other ones, the earlier ones. He had said this time things were going to be different, he would refuse her orders and stand up to her, it would be a new start, but he was weak and she was so strong. He felt the deep knife cuts around his neck where the Mistress had punished him.

He pulled his head from beneath the sacking and could see the first bright shafts of dawn sunlight spear through the pig's bladder stretched over the barn's broken window. He could see she was still sobbing and whimpering through the gag as she clawed at the dirty blindfold. He looked down at her hair flowing over his hands, silky and full of life, kissing his skin. It's what drew him to her in the first place, her long fair hair.

They must always be young, that's what the Mistress had said, because the younger girls have good strong bones for boiling to make the glue for the Bible, The Bone Bible.

She told him she knew everything because she was learned and wise, even what the Frenchman was thinking.

He stood up and looked down on the girl lying on the dry straw, dressed in blue jeans and a white blouse. It was wrong what he was doing, he knew that, but he lived for the rush he felt, the excitement. But he would suffer afterwards. He would always experience the downside, the anger of failure, knowing he was only fooling himself. He couldn't change. He was too weak.

His throat was dry and his breathing sharp as he began to shake violently. He was starting to remember the other times, the other tiny faces. He slid his hand into his deep coat pocket and felt the coldness and dampness of the long sticky boning knife blade in its nest of fine long hair. He started to remember the praise she had given him for helping her, 'You are my rock Frenchie, without you I could never construct my Bone Bible, a record of all the bones we have collected'.

The light, more intense now, streaked in and it saddened him to see her in such distress, seeing her pulling against the ropes. He raised his hands above his eyes and started to examine them. How can two such ordinary stumpy little bloodstained hands have so much power, he thought, as he started to hold her down to show her he was in control. He noticed his finger was bleeding and so put it in his mouth and licked, knowing he had been careless when he had felt the sharp blade.

Suddenly he noticed a shadow on the barn's wall and could see she was standing in the doorway.

The Mistress was becoming impatient, drawing up one of the huge boots fastened to her leg bones with iron clamps. She was now clawing at the straw covered wooden floor with the metal feet braces.

She would nod her hood towards him to signal to finish it and if he hesitated she would show her face, poke it out from the black silk hood as a final warning.

Deep down he hated her for the things she had made him do. In her native Iceland she had been known as 'The Ice Monster' due to being stranded on the Ice Mountain in record low temperatures.

She was utterly repulsive, her face neck and head were deeply pockmarked, so she appeared to be wearing a tight fitting hood that covered her face and dropped to her shoulders.

Where her nose had once sat was now a bifurcated hole, constantly oozing a green pus, in response to the guttural sound of her breathing.

She had lost her hands and feet and improvised with a selection of different attachments.

Gerta Magnusdottir, The Mistress, was getting more impatient, pulling from her claw hand the black sealskin handmade glove her father had sent her. In anger she had thrown it into the nearby bushes.

'Finish it', she ordered and then turned and left.

The Bone Bible

Chapter One

TRAFFIC SAT BUMPER TO BUMPER ON THE ROAD LEADING INTO the Western Necropolis. The villagers and fishermen had come to send out a clear message to the Chief Inspector: one murder in our village is enough, now we need time to mourn. It had been a year to the day since the savage murder.

Detective Chief Inspector Cuthbert Durham stood with Sergeant George Bede looking first at the mound of floral tributes on poor Paddy's grave, then at the throng of people. Lastly he looked up to the surroundings, the Campsies and the rounded tops of the Dumgoyne. What he would give to be up there with his Box Brownie taking his photographs of the deer.

Cuthbert walked briskly through the main doors of Stranraer Police Station and nodded a good morning to his Desk Sergeant, Nathanial Naylor. He took the overnight Incident Sheet before he calmly walked into Inspector Dorothy Malone's small office, situated between two Written Evidence Rooms.

'Is it the same one as last time?' Dolly asked, opening the audio tape cassette player.

'I thought it was but this one is slightly different', Durham answered, sliding the tape into the cassette player and sitting down opposite her. They heard the sound of a girl sobbing and murmuring before the cessation of her breath.

'It sounds the same as the last one', Dolly said.

'The very start', Cuthbert said and pressed the play button.

'There – *birr, birr*, like a pull cord to start something,' he said, but she simply shook her head.

He went to the door and waved for Desk Sergeant Naylor to join them.

'Now Nat, you are in this video club and see plenty of films with top sound effects, so I want you to tell me if you recognise a sound', Cuthbert said starting the tape.

'*Birr Birr,*' Naylor repeated, grinning knowingly.

'A pull cord?' Cuthbert asked.

'No a bird, a tropical bird,' he scratched his chin, 'South American, but as I said before this might be some joker making a hoax call to wind you up. Can you not trace the call?'

'It's not from a conventional phone, it's from a satellite phone, but Kim Ryder, a Silk at Glasgow's High Court, says she can trace it depending on the length of the call.'

Naylor returned to his desk in time to pick up the ringing telephone.

'Yes I will tell him sir,' Naylor said as he hung up and smiled. He went back through to see Cuthbert. 'The Chief of Police, Gordon Cowley, wants you to see you sir, and he isn't happy about the Ralf Stucky court case outcome.'

Cuthbert reached for his coat and took the Bentley keys from his pocket.

'It can only mean one thing, the rape and murder charges have been thrown out through some police balls up.'

'How many times has Strathclyde Police buggered up a criminal conviction?' Dolly asked.

'This will be the third,' Cuthbert answered, 'Nat, when Sergeants Franks and Jolly come in, get them to start transforming the refectory and rest room. Somehow we have to come up with a fully operational headquarters before tomorrow morning. Gordon Cowley will have to give us these serial child abduction cases now. Glasgow was given their last chance and they have blown it.'

'Didn't Cowley keep you off the case because you were close to the first victim, Poppy?' Dolly asked.

'I think Cowley now knows I acted totally professionally with poor Poppy.'

Detective Sergeant George Bede met him as he opened the Bentley door.

'I have to go up to Glasgow George, to see the Chief; he has just confirmed that Ralf Stucky's case has being thrown out.'

'So as Glasgow has buggered up the inquiry again, will we finally get the go ahead, like you wanted in the first place?' Bede asked.

'Gordon Cowley has no choice. The inquiry is ongoing but whether the evidence on the murders of the three girls is admissible, I don't know. I will have to consult Kim.'

'Three murders but no bodies,' Bede noted.

'Go back to where we were last night, George, to the back of the City Farm,' Cuthbert ordered, taking out his pocket book. 'Nat said a young courting couple phoned it in last night, wouldn't leave their names but said they saw a young girl being dragged from an orange camper van with a spare wheel on the front, possibly a VW. She was pulled by what sounds like an animal restraint towards some hut.'

'We went up and down there last night and saw no pull or wooden buildings. It must be a hoax call,' Bede suggested

'Well just run up and down again George, you may see something in the daylight. I know the City Farm is closed down now but just have a look around.'

'You think it might be linked to these murders?' George sounded doubtful.

Cuthbert looked at his watch.

'I must see Kim Ryder at the Law Court and then Gordon Cowley so I will see you in the LD Club at twelve. Did you tell Lisa we will be working late again tonight?'

'I didn't need to sir,' he answered.